EMPIRE SHATTERED

NEAL GRANT

EMPIRE
SHATTERED

NEAL GRANT

CITIOFBOOKS, INC.
3736 Eubank NE Suite A1
Albuquerque, NM 871113579
www.citiofbooks.com
Hotline: 1 (877) 3892759
Fax: 1 (505) 9307244

Ordering Information:

Quantity sales. Special discounts are available on quantity purchases by corporations, associations, and others. For details, contact the publisher at the address above.

Printed in the United States of America.

ISBN13:   Softcover   979-8-89391-375-0

Library of Congress Control Number: 2024920878

TABLE OF CONTENTS

It is he that sitteth upon the circle of the earth, and the inhabitants thereof are as grasshoppers; that stretcheth out the heavens as a curtain, and spreadeth them out as a tent to dwell in

Isa 40:22

Prologue

Although Man had been colonizing the Galaxy for more than two hundred years, we never encountered Them until twenty-eight years ago. Individuals claimed to have been abducted by Them. Certain fringe groups worshiped Them. However, in reality, They were nothing like Man had ever dreamt.

The common thread running through the lore was their appearance. Skinny. In fact, scrawny, with long thin necks. Usually pale with large bulbous heads and large black eyes. They were almost the exact opposite.

They were generally human in form, but tall, mostly between seven-and-a-half and eight feet tall with glowing eyes. Very dark, almost appearing to have leathery, lizard-like skin minus the scales. They were broad, reminiscent of human body builders. They were also fast. Very, very fast. Cleary they were built for war.

But in all the thousands of worlds Man had colonized, in all the trillions of light years Man had traveled exploring the Galaxy, we only had one encounter with one alien species on one occasion.

Until now……..

Chapter 1

A Look into the Belly of the Beast

"Bring her around hard to the docking port," ordered Commander Young. Understand that Lawrence Young's title was strictly honorary. He was not an officer. In fact, he was not even in the military. He worked for the Argalian Trade Empire. He simply commanded this ship for the Empire. He was the boss of the other employees on the ship. HIS ship. HIS beautiful ship. Of course he didn't own it, but it was HIS none the less. HIS to command. HIS to control. The Argalian Trade Ship (ATS) Focus.

When a person in the trade empire was given command of a not-yet commissioned ship, he or she was given the privilege of naming it. Young had done so because he had risen to the top largely because of his ability to focus in a laser-like fashion on his purpose. It was his pride.

As the Focus came around to the starboard side of the derelict, a chill ran down the commander's spine. "Sir, this ship is not of known human design." reported his number one computer operator, Dan Small, who had been searching the database for a match.

Indeed it didn't look remotely familiar. All ships known to Young shared certain similar design characteristics, partially for the practical purpose of flight and technological efficiency, partially to remind us that we were all human.

What happens when twins are separated at birth and finally meet later on as adults? They meet a stranger. Such had happened to mankind.

There were entire planets of humans which had been colonized more than one hundred years earlier that didn't have a single living resident who had ever seen an off-worlder. Some of these worlds had become xenophobic toward other human beings. Perhaps that was why many ship design characteristics had undergone sweeping changes; while they reminded us that we were all parts of the same whole at the same time they enabled us to keep ourselves separated. This was an interesting study in Man's duality of mind.

The unfamiliar derelict ship resembled a model of an atom. It had an axis about two miles long which ran through its center. Approximately one-half mile from the top of the axis, a one hundred fifty foot wide circular rib protruded. The rib followed the circumference of a circle until it met with the axis again, about one-half mile from the bottom. It then jutted out the other side of the axis and did the same forming a complete ring. There were three such rings. In the center of the axis, encapsulated by the rings, were two orbs which rotated in opposite directions.

"Brian," began the Commander, "how long do you estimate this tin can has been here?" Brian Schultz was the Focus's junior scientist.

"Based on the hull's particular and moisture accumulation, I would estimate about fifteen years or so."

Young let this sink in. "All right, let's do what we do," he finally ordered.

What they did was salvage. As mankind had spread across the Galaxy, his technological abilities had grown. At the same time, so had his xenophobia. Certain factions became very territorial. Wars broke out, lots of wars. This left lots of 'stuff' out there to be recovered. 'Stuff' was an inside joke. Argolan, the founder of the Trade Empire, kept his ego in check and those of his employees by saying, "We find stuff." Simple. Perhaps a bit (intentionally) self-deprecating, but true.

In the beginning of course, it wasn't an empire at all, but a single man, his small garbage-hauling tug, and his desire for more. Thankfully, Argolan had come from a faction of humanity which was not isolationist. One can only guess if he would have been able to overcome the fears of an isolationist upbringing and build the Empire into what it had become.

"Project Team to the bridge," Young ordered over the ship-wide public address system.

As the Focus came around to the derelict's docking port, Commander Young's orders came rapid fire:

"Navigator…"

"Forward thrusters, slow to five KPH."

"Take her in nice and easy."

"Aft starboard thrusters, bring us around fifteen degrees."

"Slow to two KPH."

"Easy…..Easy…."

"Align Focus's docking port with hers."

"Extend mooring clamps."

"Roll two degrees clockwise."

"Slow to point three KPH."

"Dock!"

Young marveled. To the casual observer he have would probably looked like a navigational genius--a wonder of the art of spatial relationships. In reality, there was a computer monitor on the armrest of his commander's chair. Its screen contained a graphic depiction of the Focus and the ship with which she was in process of docking. All Young needed to do was watch the screen and issue orders. It was no more difficult than a twentieth-century video game. The computer would even offer course correction recommendations. Young marveled at how dependent Mankind had become on his machines.

Young called on the intercom to the dock engineering room, "Erect force field around Focus's dock, configuration Alpha." Alpha was the code for the standard controlled area, a sterile environment created by force field walls and ceiling. Another force field enabled the opening of the docking hatches without the possibility of ship-wide contamination. If a contaminant were to have entered the controlled area, it would have been detected by the stand alone air-filtration system. If it were a live contaminant, it would have been destroyed by ultra violet emitters, inanimate, it would have been destroyed by the laser emitters. Configuration Alpha meant the controlled area would have been of dimensions large enough to accommodate a project crew of twelve for seventy-two hours. The A-configuration contained a drafting table with a work console on which the project manager was able to develop project plans, two science stations (one with a metallurgical station) for team scientists; a standard armory; a scanning station for Intel personnel; spacesuits for the entire team; a rest room, water, rations and enough air reserve for the team to survive for those seventy-two hours during which they would inhabit the controlled area.

The dock engineering team was responsible for assembling the controlled area, while at the same time, the docking team director, David Stein, tracked thousands of metrics relating to the integrity of the dock connection. Stein marveled. There were hundreds of factors that went into maintaining integrity of a strong dock, and unfortunately, the whole was greater than the sum of its parts. There was an intuitive component to it. For years, man had attempted to write computer programs to do this job just to meet with disaster after disaster. Stein marveled at how, with all of the incredible machines mankind had created over the last few centuries, he had needed to remain completely able to operate independently of them.

This was Stein's value on the open market. There weren't many men in the Galaxy capable of performing Stein's job at his level. He was actually the highest paid person in the Focus's crew. Part of Stein's success had been to hire great managers. While he watched the metrics, he was able to keep his mind clear enough to sense docking integrity stresses because he had the best managers in the industry to lead their teams in setting up the controlled area autonomously. Simultaneously Stein's mind consciously processed thousands of metrics per second. Stein's ability to multi-task to this degree was a result of the people on his home planet having developed an immense ability for mental acumen and sharpness.

At last the project team arrived on the bridge, and Young led them into his briefing chamber so they could discuss their project plan.

Three hours later, Commander Young and the project team assembled in the dock engineering room. "I want this done by regulation--no mistakes, no accidents," Young began. "I want everyone to return safely."

With that, a door opened at the entry end of a force-field-created hallway which led to the controlled area. Once the entire project team had entered the hallway, they were scanned with several low-intensity lasers. The team was now becoming part of the controlled area. After about forty-five minutes of scans the computer chimed the go-ahead, and the force field at the end of the hallway dropped. The team-members went to earn their pay.

Steve Johnson, the project manager, immediately went to work at his drafting table, while simultaneously the science team went to the door to begin scanning. Johnson started his questioning.

"What are the door dimensions?"

The science team put an object which looked like a coin about the size of a silver dollar with four equidistant protrusions that looked like pencil tips near the center of the door. One protrusion pointed up, one down, one left and one right. Brian Schultz, the team's chief scientist, pushed on the center of the 'coin', and an infrared laser shot out of each of the protrusions. Each beam extended to one edge of the door, stopping abruptly at that edge unaided. The tool chirped and gave the dimensional feedback metrics to Johnson.

"What is the door thickness?"

Abraham Kalman, the team's director of science, put a rectangular object on the door. After a few moments of humming the machine became silent. Kalman pulled it from the door and looked at the information on the display. "No information available," he said incredulously' "We can't scan through the material."

"Any metrics on the composition?"

"Scan picked up trace amounts of titanium, aluminum, lead and.....Sodium?! But that is only about five percent of the mass. The rest is unrecognizable." Kalman had never seen anything like this.

Johnson thought for a few moments. "Okay, let's do it the old-fashioned way."

With that, the science team removed the 'coin' and Mickey Overton, the team's machine operator/machinist, came forward with various power tools. The first tool was used to attempt to cut the door's surface. Nothing. The second shot a force field at the door. At first the force field hit the door with the equivalent of two hundred pounds of pressure. The team had to start lightly, because the job right now was only to study the door, not to open it before they had donned their space suits. Next they shot five hundred pounds. Then one thousand. Then four thousand. Overton adjusted the tool to maximum setting. This setting sent a shockwave at the door with the equivalent of nine thousand five hundred pounds of pressure. Not even a dent.

The third tool was a standard laser drill. Mickey Overton drilled for nearly three-quarters of an hour. Nothing. "Sir, I don't know what in the world this thing is made if. It resists cutting, blunt force and my drill attempts."

Johnson became a bit agitated by his team's apparent lack of progress. "Erect a type-S force field four point eight nanometers above the surface of the door," he ordered while referencing his copy of the project plan.

A type-S force field measured topographical or surface qualities. It had a feedback tension system which took constant readings. It worked like this: The field was comprised of a screen of billions of beams which would run over the surface of an object alternately from left to right and from right to left. The field was also comprised of a screen of billions of beams running over the object's surface alternately from top to bottom and from bottom to top. Wherever anything protruded from the surface, the beams running in all four directions broke and the precise location and dimensions of the broken beams were sent to the project team's computer.

Immediately, the computer chirped, and a very small area on the purple force field began to glow bright green indicating where the surface imperfection was. Overton came back with a new laser tool. With the guidance of the type-S force field, he began to cut. Off it came. The team now had a sample of the metal of which the hatch was comprised to study. After about an hour of metallurgical study, the science team gave their reports to the project team.

"Nothing. We can't scan it. We can't see what it's made of. The only chemical interaction we could create was with sulfuric acid, which by the way, would not corrode it appreciably. With the acid, we were able to create microscopic pockets of hydrogen in the outermost layer of the door. I can't see this being of any use," Kalman finished his report.

"Why hydrogen?" asked Lance Charles, head of the security group for the project team.

"Hydrogen is one of the gas by-products of sulfuric acid as a result of corrosion," responded Johnson. Then turning back to Kalman, he declared, "You said the corrosion was not significant."

"No. It would take weeks for our acids to eat through the door if it were only one-quarter of an inch thick. Of course we don't know how thick it is because our scanners can't penetrate it."

"Something dawned on me," said Johnson. "You said there were trace amounts of lead in the door. Lead expands greatly when cooled. Can we get some temperature conductivity through the door's alloy? If we can perhaps we can use this to our advantage"

Kalman went over to the metallurgical station and returned about twenty minutes later. "Yes," he said.

The two men mulled over what they knew. After a long period of silence, Kalman smiled and said, "I have a thought. What if we introduced a layer of sulfuric acid across the surface of the door? Let it seep down into the surface pores of the material to create the hydrogen bubbles. Then we could cool the door with a hypothermic beam. The hydrogen will turn to liquid and expand somewhat, but more importantly, it will conduct the cold into the door. In the layer beneath the hydrogen pockets, the lead will expand from the cold of the hydrogen and the hypothermic beam. Perhaps we can cause the expanding lead to 'knock away' the outer layer of alloy with the hydrogen pockets almost as a bottle of water left out in freezing temperatures bursts the bottle as the water freezes and expands. This could knock away the outer layer of the door. Then we could repeat the process with the new outer layer of door. And then do it again and again, kind of a chemical chisel." After Kalman had laid out his idea there were a few chuckles and even some wisecracks about his possibly waning sanity.

Nonetheless, Kalman went back to his computer workstation. After a few minutes of computer modeling, Kalman remarked, "It could work. But this would have to be a scientific process and may take many tries. We would have to take metrics of the reaction after each attempt created and eventually we could possibly find a way to make this work. It is a long shot, however."

"Any better ideas?" Johnson asked team.

No response.

"Let's do it." Johnson ordered

Kalman was right. The process was slow and tedious. It took more than twelve hours of trial and error before they had even a small result, but once they had their first success, the process achieved a fast track. They had needed to introduce other chemicals into the mix as well as adjust some of the other variables.

The door was now open, and Johnson's team, wearing their spacesuits, was the first crew to ever look into the belly of an alien space ship. As it turned out, the door was only one-sixteenth of an inch thick.

Chapter 2

A Silent Meeting

As Admiral James Masse approached the designated rendezvous location his hands trembled. Imagine the admiral over the Fifth Fleet of the strongest military power in the history of the Galaxy being part of such a seedy scene. He donned casual attire in an attempt to remain anonymous, but he still felt as though he was attracting attention.

When the communication from Zahn had arrived, Masse had immediately withdrawn his command ship from the effort in which it was engaged and brought it here to Sigma One. Sigma One was a trading planet in a solar system of trading planets. Many low-lifes lived here, even in the most affluent sections. Now here he was, an admiral, in the crusty underbelly of a seedy world, but it was worth it, for the honor he would bring to the Fifth Fleet for finally bringing down his prey.

The alley was just off of the main street of Capital City. Surrounded by unsightly characters, Masse kept his head buried in the upright collar of his tan trench coat and just continued to walk. There was trash everywhere on the ground. As the admiral rounded the corner and headed into the dark alley, rats scattered. The filth! Not becoming of a naval officer.

When Masse reached the end of the alley he turned around and looked for Zahn, but he was nowhere to be seen. Masse turned over a broken crate, bottom up, and sat, reflecting on how he had gotten to this point. Just then Zahn and one of his henchmen stepped from the shadows.

Zahn eyeballed Masse without saying a word. He could see a bulge under Zahn's left armpit beneath his coat. A gun. Continuing the silence, Zahn's companion extended his right hand. In it was an envelope with a seal. Masse extended his right hand. In it was a vial containing... well... something more valuable to Zahn than money. Once the exchange was complete Masse turned around and walked away without a word ever being said.

As Masse's shuttle launched from the Capital City Port he kicked back in the cabin, leaving the flying up to his personal pilot; a fringe benefit of being an admiral. He opened the envelope being careful not to damage its contents. As he read the document a smile came to his lips. "Gotcha, you miserable excuse for a human being."

Masse pressed the button on his intercom and said, "Captain Rydell, call the Warship Deference and tell Captain Donohue to set a course for the Galafon System. Oh, and signal my command ship to rendezvous there with us as well, have them bring three more fleet warships with them. "

This was going to be sweet.

Chapter 3

The Return Home

After hours of lying awake in bed, Commander Julian Paul had just fallen asleep when the intercom beckoned, "Julian, we are entering orbit of Sharanda. We have been authorized to use Launch Corridor Gamma in seventeen minutes." On the other end of the intercom was Julian's Crew Manager Gabriel Williams. The two men had known each other for more than twenty-seven of Paul's thirty-three years. He was a good man. Paul had strong faith in his abilities and integrity. They had been educated in Trade Empire schools as both of their fathers worked for the Trade Empire. Rather, Gabriel's father worked for the Trade Empire, Julian's father owned the Trade Empire.

"All right Gabriel, I'll be down in a few minutes," Julian almost whined. The ATS Liahona had been out in deep space nearly four months. Because of the current hostilities between Ranis and Embuieck, there had been a lot of 'stuff' to find in their shared solar system. Julian had been working twenty-two-hour days almost non-stop during these past four months. Only now during the trip home had he enjoyed any downtime, but he was still exhausted.

Julian rolled onto his left side and reaching over his head, grabbed his journal from his bookshelf. Journaling was an exercise that Argolan had taught him which had become a daily habit. He penned a few thoughts, and upon finishing, tossed his journal back to its resting place.

Julian sat up and looked around his quarters, happily contemplating the thought that he wouldn't have to sleep here again for a long time. His quarters were modest, almost overly so. Although he couldn't see it due to his distorted self image, Julian was a man of extraordinary strength of character. He was fiercely loyal to his crew, and in spite of his extraordinary wealth, he had always tried to be one of the crew. And he was. Most of his crew would have died by his command. They loved him with a bond like that of brothers.

Julian stood up, crossed the room and reached into his closet to pull out a shirt and pants to throw on over his undergarments. Of course it was only a few steps across the dark room. His quarters were always quite dark. He actually slept with the same light level he used during his waking periods. There was a single twin bed with a bookcase headboard against the wall opposite the closet. He was an avid reader, and when his team left on a mission, he would grab books from his father's library, relocating them to his bookcase.

Julian stopped and took a moment to study the most important items on his bookshelf which were kept at pillow level, pictures of his family. There was a picture of him and Argolan, a picture of him and his sister Faith, (Argolan's daughter),and a picture of him and his parents when he was five years old. Looking at the pictures, Julian's thoughts drifted to his parents. They had been miners on Etty Prime when mankind's one chance encounter with an alien race occurred.

It was a beautiful, sunny spring morning. Julian and some of the other miners' children were out running in the valley, something they often did in nice weather. Suddenly the sky grew dark. The children looked up to see dozens of ships each the size of a large city descending from the sky. The children scattered. While the other children headed toward the miner's camp, Julian found a rock formation at the base of one of the hills on the south end of the valley. He watched from his hiding place as, off in the distance, enormous aliens began to pour out of bays of the landed craft.

The aliens sprinted from their craft and ran out of the valley heading toward the mining settlement in perfect military formation.

Julian prayed as his parents had taught him for the courage to act and save the settlement, but to no avail.

Julian began hearing laser blasts and screams off in the distance. It had taken these beasts only a few minutes to reach the settlement which lay nestled in the hills over a mile and a half away.

They killed everyone. No one was left except the hidden Julian. As quickly as they had run to the settlement, the aliens returned, still in perfect formation. They boarded their ships which subsequently took off.

Of course Julian had relatively little memory of these events because he was so young when they occurred. It was hazy at best. Almost like a dream. However one part of this memory was still sharp, like the blade of a knife piercing his side......

Guilt. Cowardice.

He remembered being paralyzed by fear, not understanding why the Lord had not provided him with the courage to act. He had hidden like a coward, not able to run home. Perhaps if he hadn't frozen he would have been able to do something, to help. Maybe he could have saved his parents, friends and the some of the other miners.

When Julian's thoughts returned to the present he finished dressing and strolled up to the bridge. Every employee he passed in the hallway greeted him with a big smile and a warm hello. When he finally entered the bridge, Gabriel took notice of him and stood from the commander's chair saying, "Julian, we are just about to make port. ETA three minutes."

Julian always got goose bumps watching the approach to a planet from the bridge. Seeing what looked at first like a spec of dust on the other end of the Galaxy, watching it grow larger and eventually becoming all that could be seen was an awesome sight. Making port at Sharanda was quite different from making port elsewhere. Sharanda was quite common in that it was a relatively barren, mountainous, desert-planet. However, its quotidian topography was eclipsed by its one unique feature.

Sharanda emitted an anomalous energy field. While some scientists believed this to be caused by a mixture of chemicals in the sand coupled with massive amounts of subsurface ores and a unique type of radiation created by Sharanda's sun, no one had been able to prove it scientifically. Whatever the cause, the net result was a disruption of the energy field created by anti-gravity thrusters, the type of thrusters used to land and launch light-speed-enabled craft. So while these ships were capable of flying to Sharanda, they simply couldn't land on Sharanda, rendering it valueless to mankind.

This was part of Argolan's genius. He hired a top-secret team of scientists who developed a radically advanced force field technology. This technology was then used to create a group of specialized force field corridors to block the energy field. The corridors extended from the launch hangers on Sharanda all the way out into space like altitudinous skyscrapers preventing the disruptive energy from affecting the thrusters of ships traveling within, thus allowing them to land on and launch from Sharanda. Technology like these shields had never been seen before. It was groundbreaking, unprecedented.

This was part of Argolan's genius. While *his* light speed vessels could land on Sharanda, *no one else's* were able to, thus preventing the Argalian Trade Empire's facilities from ever being attacked by pirates or other foes. Pirates typically raided by jumping near to their prey on a light speed burst, attacking them and then fleeing on another light speed burst. This couldn't be done to Sharanda. Moreover, an aerial bombardment of Sharanda by laser cannon was not feasible because its energy field would dissipate a laser blast long before it could make landfall.

This was part of Argolan's genius. For years no one would go near Sharanda. Mankind assumed it was of no value because the same light speed ships that would be required to bring people to Sharanda could never land on it. Argolan had vision enough to see that what all of the rest of mankind considered to be Sharanda's greatest detriment was actually its greatest asset.

Julian watched Sharanda gradually grow larger through the forward viewer. After a few moments he was able to make out Mount

Efil. Home. An added layer of security. The Argalian Trade Empire was headquartered within Mount Efil.

While Sharanda was impervious to aerial bombardment by energy weapons, conventional weapons were a different story. Conventional rocket, jet and combustion engines were not affected by the energy field on Sharanda, so a bombardment by rockets could be carried out on the planet's surface. Argolan, knowing the Trade Empire would cultivate enemies one day, built his Trade Empire's base of operations into a hollowed out mountain. This fortress was virtually impenetrable to conventional weaponry.

The facility was enormous, stretching for hundreds of miles north to south and more than twelve miles east to west. All of the employees and families of employees working for the Trade Empire lived within the facility. They were free to come and go as they pleased, even to explore Sharanda. Of course there wasn't much to see. Besides, Argolan had built such a tight-knit community that most of the time the fifty-plus thousand families living in Mount Efil were content to engage in leisure activities together while not working.

As Julian watched Sharanda take over the expanse of the viewer, he grew homesick. He had missed his father while away for these past four months. He always missed him, but this time it had been especially hard. Argolan had turned sixty in Julian's absence. Over the last ten years Julian had watched as his father had grown old and relatively frail. Well, relatively for Argolan. Argolan had always been a hulk of a man, an avid exerciser who ate healthfully. But in these past ten years things had changed.

Control of the Galactic Democratic Republic, which had once been the constitutionally governing body of the Galaxy, had been subverted.

The courts, which were supposed to be the final power to hold government to its constitutionally appointed powers, crumbled. Activist judges, who had taken an oath to uphold the Galactic constitution, ignored their sworn duties to interpret the Constitution's text. Instead these judges began to interpret, even to bend, the Constitution based on their own Galactic view, using rhetoric such as, "If the framers of the Constitution were alive today," or "When the framers wrote the Constitution they couldn't have foreseen this," to justify their actions.

Without a court system to hold it in check, congress went on a power-driven frenzy to regulate as much of day-to-day life and commerce as possible. Life became so complex that almost no one could operate, even on a personal level without legal counsel. Lawsuits became as common as colds. Trial lawyers, and more importantly the Lawyer's Guild, became the wealthiest and largest force in the Galaxy. That was when the Guild made its move.

Elected legislators and candidates for office who were loyal to the Republic and unwilling to embrace the tenets of the Guild became targets. The Lawyer's Guild attacked them one by one, dragging them, often frivolously, into court. With the Guild's endless financial and legal-counsel resources, it was able to perpetuate lawsuits indefinitely, binding candidates who would not support the Guild's agenda. Over time, the intimidation of free-thinking legislators and candidates became so overt, no one would run against the candidates beholden to the Guild.

Eventually, man's desire to accept personal responsibility atrophied. Businesses shrank from all endeavors which could lead to liability. Like an army marching from country to country as it invaded, so went the lawyers, attacking industry after industry while they invaded.

Citizens of the Galactic Democratic Republic, which had been modeled after the government of the United States on Old Earth, should have learned from history. Just as in the first half of the twenty-first century the United States experienced a crippling of commerce due to rampant litigation, so had the Galactic Democratic Republic.

As this happened, mankind had two choices. First, people could rise up and rebel, but it didn't happen. This is a typical story told throughout the Scriptures. God's people would grow in righteousness. They would gain great knowledge, wisdom and wealth. Next they would become proud and fall away from living by the Lord's laws. They would become apathetic and then eventually become enslaved. It was a cycle as old as time. The second choice, to submit to this oppression, was the path of least resistance. So while the Galactic Democratic Republic still stood, it was in name only. The core of the Republic, which was individual liberty, had been eroded by the subversive lust for power and control of the Lawyer's Guild.

The Lawyer's Guild had not directly attacked the Trade Empire. However, laws governing salvage and trade had become so convoluted that the business had become impractical. It was only because of its already massive success that the Trade Empire was able to go on. However, in the Trade Empire's heyday, Argolan had at one point employed more than one hundred twenty-five thousand people. His profit had been so diluted he was now down to about eighty thousand. He just couldn't support any more. This wore on him. It had aged him at a rate that alarmed Julian and Faith. Julian broke from his thoughts and watched his home approach.

"Julian, we have clearance to enter the Corridor," reported the navigations manager.

"Proceed," Julian replied half-heartedly as he thought of home.

"Back again," Julian thought. The Liahona had brought him back again. The ATS Liahona had been named after a device which the Ancients had received from the Lord. It had guided them safely to the land Covenanted to them by the Father. The promise of the ATS Liahona was that she would always bring her crew home safely.

Chapter 4

Reunion

While Julian made his way through the hallways of Mount Efil, he further reminisced about his childhood. He and his friends would run for hours through these halls playing games. His favorite had always been war. But unlike games of war that had been played on Old Earth, these games were played with real guns. Stunners actually. They would give one a nice jolt but do no harm. The rise of these games among Julian's generation here had helped to make the current workforce of the Trade Federation as battle-hardened as it was. Brilliant battle strategists were everywhere. The young men had grown into strong men who wouldn't back down from a fight.

But these were not Julian's fondest memories. Those were of him and his father playing games such as hide and seek or tag. Of course, whenever Argolan caught him, a battle of tickling fingers would ensue. He had many great memories. Then the soberness of reality crept back into Julian's consciousness. How much would Argolan have deteriorated since last they saw each other?

Arrived at the door of Argolan's quarters, Julian stopped and prayed quietly. Although Julian prayed, he didn't expect much. He had found having faith to be a challenge ever since that day on Etty Prime. Nonetheless he went through the motions in which he had been trained.

Argolan, who was a man of great faith, had always tried to help Julian acquire the power of faith for himself, but he was only left with fear and guilt. Nonetheless Julian prayed to not show signs of dismay about Argolan's appearance in his presence. When he finished he entered as Argolan had always instructed.

Argolan almost always kept the door to his quarters unlocked and encouraged his team members to enter without knocking. He had always wanted to be there for his people, something many people who start companies tended to forget as their organizations grew, instituting a "closed door" or "by appointment only" policy. Julian had caught onto this and had run with it. He really lived like the average people in Efil. This was not quite the case with Argolan.

Argolan's quarters were mammoth. The receiving room/living room was about two thousand square feet. It had five hallways leading out of it like spokes on a wheel: One to the bedroom, a very plush, elegant bedroom, one to a gymnasium which contained a private pool, one to an entertainment complex with a full-size movie theater, one to a game room and one to a Sacred Room.

Some criticized Argolan for his lifestyle but he had earned it. He had gone bankrupt numerous times before achieving financial success. He had had debtors send mercenaries after him to collect his head for a debt (he eventually paid every cent back to everyone from whom he had borrowed money). He had spent years working day and night to build his organization. He had employed hundreds of thousands of people and had paid them all fair wages, increasing their lifestyles. He had also brought unprecedented prosperity to a section of the Galaxy which had been on the brink of extinction before he came. Abundant with poverty and crime, the influx of Argolan's well-paid employees reinvigorated the economy of Sharanda's solar system as well as those of surrounding systems. Argolan had earned his lifestyle and had improved the lives of many others in the process.

This portion of the Galaxy owned a certain characteristic which made growth and expansion very difficult: the Norson Expanse. The Norson Expanse was a field of stellar debris suspended in a gravity depression. This field of intense gravity was created by the competing pull of dual bodies. On one end of the expanse was a white dwarf named Augustine, while on the other end, the end nearest to Sharanda's system, was the Blanner Black Hole. The gravity depression trapped matter inside it, suspending it there, creating a natural barrier between the Old Territories (on Old Earth's side of the Expanse) and the New Territories (on Sharanda's side of the Expanse).

While modern day anti-gravity shield-tuning techniques made travel through the expanse possible (but still dangerous,) through travel had not been feasible a few years prior. As a result, Old Earth's government had never extended its infrastructure into the New Territories. Earliest settlers of the New Territories had circumnavigated the enormous anomaly, which cost them many years. The natural result of this barrier had been that the Galaxy had grown into two separate entities: the Old Territories, now governed by the Galactic Constitutional Republic (which had been subverted by the Lawyer's Guild) and the New Territories. Because it was technically under the jurisdiction of the Republic, the New Territories didn't have an official unifying, governing body of its own. However, in practical terms, the Republic's control did not extend beyond the Norson Expanse with any great fortitude. In fact, because of the great expense to the Republic to build infrastructure in the New Territories, the only regulatory arm of the Republic there was the Sigma Commerce Bureau, whose power of enforcement was quite limited for a region this large. Resultantly, this corner of the Galaxy was instead held together by interdependent commerce and trade.

Argolan was nowhere to be seen. However, if he was in his quarters, Julian knew where he would find him. He went quietly through the door leading to the Sacred Room. Upon entering the Sacred Room he felt a tremendous peace come over him. He had forgotten how beautiful it was. The room had extremely tall ceilings and walls painted white with off-white highlights. The furniture was beautiful and light-colored. In the center of the ceiling hung a huge crystal chandelier. A gorgeous cathedral window was set into one of the walls.

What always struck Julian about the Sacred Room was that no matter how much tumult there was outside, this room was always separated from it. Julian imagined that if there was a heaven, this was a close facsimile.

As he moved from the back of the room, Julian saw Argolan kneeling in prayer at the front of the room facing away from him. Julian hesitated before continuing forward. As Julian neared Argolan, Argolan spoke, startling Julian who thought he had approach noiselessly.

"Reports of your excursion appear profitable, son."

"Very, father." With that, Argolan swiftly rose to his feet, whirled sprinted forward and embraced Julian. Unfortunately, Julian was astonished by his father's appearance, unable to conceal it.

Argolan smiled, "You like the makeover?"

Julian was so stunned that he was speechless. His father looked wonderful, appearing just as he had twenty years earlier. When he finally regained his composure, Julian croaked, "What happened?"

"To make a long story short, I was given a healing blessing by two elders. It cleared my mind of the fog that has hung over me for the last decade. I am reinvigorated. I started to work out again, changed my diet and voilà!"

Tears streamed down Julian's face. Argolan smirked, "Don't worry. You'll still inherit my Empire.....SOMEDAY!!"

"Father, I expected to be burying you in the near future. I.... I didn't know how I would go on."

"Son, you're strong."

"No, I'm not. Since the day that you found me on Etty Prime, you have breathed that strength into my life. Without you I would be nothing more than that frightened five-year-old."

Argolan boomed sternly, "That's nonsense! Watching you grow and mature over past…huh, almost thirty years, has been the most amazing experience of my life. I have raised you well. Do not deny me credit, but you have run with it. You are a strong man."

Chapter 5

A Heading

Captain Donahue sat across the briefing table from Admiral Masse. Donahue, a short, heavy, dark complected man, with a shaved head and a goatee, was dwarfed by the hulking admiral.

"But sir," Donahue persisted, "Without any intention of questioning your orders, I am simply wondering why we have changed course. It is enough of an oddity that we made a stop in the Sigma System, but now a course change that contradicts our orders! Can you enlighten me in any way?"

"You are a remarkably astute young officer," offered Masse. He had learned how to stroke egos over the course of his career. That was a large part of how he had risen to where he was. "These questions are well in line. I come to your warship on my private shuttle and for all intents and purposes, commandeer it. And now I issue an order that supersedes your prior orders and issue a 'no external communications' order at the same time. Your concern is well-founded. My behavior is highly unusual."

Donahue nodded as if to say thank you for a compliment.

Masse continued, "What I am about to tell you is classified. Naval Command sent me to Sigma to take possession of documents that could shift the political and economic balance of the Galaxy. There I met with Sigma Commerce Bureau agents who gave me a report."

The "Sigma Commerce Bureau" contacts of whom Masse spoke were actually mercenaries whom Masse used clandestinely from time to time, not representatives of the Commerce Bureau. This Masse knew. Today they had delivered him a forged report. This Masse didn't know.

He continued, "This report details illegal salvage operations in the Ranis System performed by the ATS Liahona."

With this Donahue grew skeptical but didn't show it outwardly, not wanting to expose his hand. All Naval officers were aware of the antipathy between Masse and Argolan. Years before they had been good friends, but something had occurred, and, no one except Argolan and Masse knew exactly what that was.

"That's Julian Paul's ship," Donahue said, attempting to show no emotion. "Sir, isn't this a legal matter, something better left to law enforcement?"

"Normally it would be, but these orders come from the President himself, and I won't question them" Masse lied. Another skill he had developed over the years. Another skill that had helped him rise to where he was. "If the Trade Federation were to fall, it could shift the social, economic and political structure of the Galafon System, which is the gateway between the Old and New Territories. If chaos were to erupt in the Galafon System, it could have Galaxy-wide ramifications."

Donahue's stomach dropped, as a result of the terror he felt, but maintained his poker face. If the President had so ordered, the Lawyer's Guild was behind it with an ulterior motive. Everything they touched had the stench of politics. "How did I wind up involved in this mess?" Donahue wondered. He had joined the armed forces willingly, even proudly. But he had done so to defend the Republic.

Unfortunately, a disconcerting trend had been evolving in the military in the past ten to fifteen years. Convinced they were upholding the Republic, much of the military's hierarchy had become loyal to the Guild in that era. Donahue, however, could see through the Guild. The lawyers were slowly subverting the Republic, causing it to atrophy from within, while at the same time, intruding and weighing it down with endless bureaucracy.

"How did I wind up involved in this mess?" Donahue wondered.

"Besides," Masse continued, "I think that the Lawyer's Guild would like to keep this out of the media. The Lawyer's Guild has stayed pretty much away from the Trade Federation over the years, legalizing, but not cripplingly-so, the salvage industry. To be sure, it has put some pressure on salvage operations in the Galaxy, but not compared to other industries. If word of this were to get out, it might not bode well for them in regard to public image. That is probably the main reason the military is being used for this mission. It is also why I have put the 'no outside communications' order in place"

Once again, a sense of dread forced its way into Donahue's consciousness. This was work for an ambassadorial contingent, not a military ship. This was way out of a naval crew's league.

"What will stop one of the crew from alerting the media that something is afoot after your communications ban has been lifted?"

Masse responded, "Orders. Besides, by that time, our business there will have concluded, and it will make no difference if the media is alerted.

"Oh, by the way, we'll be rendezvousing with my command ship and three of the Fifth Fleet's other warships just outside of the Galafon System."

"Great," Donahue thought, "We're expecting a fight."

Chapter 6

A Secret Conversation

Even before Donohue reached his quarters he knew that he was going to disregard Masse's orders. Others in the Fifth Fleet followed him blindly. In fact, they almost worshipped him. And why not? Masse was the most highly decorated man in the history of the Navy. He was a brilliant strategist, a rugged warrior and so charismatic that one wanted to follow where he led, even to his own demise.

In truth, Masse had achieved more success in the military than most officers would ever even dream of. But to Donohue, this was irrelevant for two reasons. First, in spite of desiring to follow Masse, his actions departed too far from due course. Donohue *wanted* to follow Masse's orders blindly, but his logical side forbade him. Second, Donohue had his own set of orders.

Donohue entered his quarters, crossed the room and reached up over his bed to remove the frame that hung on the wall. The frame contained a Smith and Wesson M&P nine-millimeter conventional firearm. It was an invaluable antique. Donohue turned the frame over and extracted the four screws which held the back in place. Once the back was removed, he unscrewed the mounts that held the pistol in place. Donahue then released the weapon from its mounts and disengaged its clip. He slid two bullets out of the clip exposing an opening below. Next Donohue pushed a button on the back of the clip, and a video screen the size of a matchbook cover popped out of the top of the clip like the blade of a stiletto knife.

Donohue tapped the screen and a dark figure with piercing grey eyes appeared on it.

"Report," the figure ordered.

Donohue ran through the whole scenario including his most recent conversation with Masse.

The figure clearly became angry. "You need to mask any aggressive feelings you may have here. Remember your orders."

"But," Donohue pled in an almost whiney voice, "This course of action was completely unanticipated."

"We anticipated it," responded the figure.

"But how?" queried Donohue.

"Do you think that you are the only observer we have?" asked the figure, in a belittling tone. "We have far more useful observers within the Fifth Fleet as well as within the Trade Federation."

Donohue was taken aback. "I don't understand"

"You don't need to understand. Just follow your orders. Don't fail us, the Republic is counting on you."

The screen went dark. Donohue shuddered. There was no telling to what lengths these people would go to see their plans brought to fruition.

While Donohue returned his transmitter to its hiding place, he reflected upon his orders, simply to observe Masse, not to interfere and then to report back regularly to his contact with the eyes, the contact whose name he didn't even know. All Donohue had wanted to do as long as he could remember was to serve the Galactic Constitutional Government and be a model soldier. Now he was entangled in this mess.

Chapter 7

Young's Transmission

After many more days of rest in his modest quarters on Sharanda, Julian lay on his bed looking up at the ceiling when the intercom beeped, "Julian, please come to the Ops Center." The Operations Center, also called the Ops Center or the Command Center, was the part of Mount Efil from where the Empire was run. Communications as well as business operations were largely developed and disseminated from there.

While strolling down to the Ops Center, Julian stopped several times to talk with friends and acquaintances. He had not seen any of them in more than four months. It was good to be home. At the Ops Center, Julian was greeted with big smiles and many embraces. Argolan, who was waiting there for him, looked like a child on Christmas morning. He couldn't contain himself. "You're not going to believe this."

"Believe what?" Julian asked, starting to feel a bit excited himself.

"The Focus has been out since well before you left."

"I assumed that she had come back months ago. Why was she out so long for a simple run to Sigma Six?" inquired Julian.

"That's just it. When she arrived at the Sigma System her sensors picked up an anomaly the likes of which we have never seen before."

"An anomaly?"

"An energy signature. Very weak, but unlike anything we have ever seen before. When the daily activities report came in via wave from the

Focus, it caught my attention. Perhaps it was the Spirit talking to me or perhaps just my finely tuned intuition, I ordered Commander Young to investigate."

"You had them break flight plan, father? It must have been a pretty strong feeling, but where is this going?"

"They did it."

"Did what?!" Julian said, rather irked at the game of cat-and-mouse.

Julian had always possessed an insatiable curiosity, which he had never learned to temper with patience.

"Found an alien vessel. Alien technology. The works but no corpses. The Focus will have a communications window in a few minutes, and I knew you would want to be among the first here to see her newly acquired cargo." .

For the next few minutes, Julian visited with the various members of the Trade Federation Ops crew, most of whom he had known since he was a little child. His mind, however, was not on the conversations in which he engaged. He was tingling with excitement. This was huge. It was groundbreaking. In reality, he was the only human being ever to have seen an alien and lived to tell about it, but he had never thought of it as "groundbreaking." or "extraordinary." It was more….painful.

And again the knife blade dug into his side.

"Coward."

He pushed the blade back into the shadows of his mind where he had attempted to keep it hidden for the past twenty eight-eight years. A beep from the communications computer interrupted Julian's torment drawing his attention to the Ops Center viewer. On it appeared Commander Young.

Argolan smiled. "It sounds as though congratulations are in order, Commander."

Young returned the smile. "Thank you, Argolan. In reality, any accolades should go to you. I was prepared to go about my business on Sigma Six. It was because of your directive that the Focus pursued this gold mine."

"Tell me about your inventory."

"Begin feed," Smith ordered his communications manager. After a brief delay, a video feed flickered onto the viewer displaying one item after another. Julian concentrated so hard on the video that he didn't hear Commander Young reporting his science team's appraisals of the items to Argolan.

"……and these we found four hundred fifteen decks below the docking port in what we presume was a medical lab."

The video panned to what looked like a food synthesizer and perhaps eating implements. "These three items are from what was probably the mess hall.

"This keypad like device was found in what we surmise to have been the commander's quarters." The device had what appeared to be a small hologram emitter, a button and sixteen keys with what appeared to be alien symbols on them.

Next the video moved to what were doubtless weapons. Amongst them were guns, grenades, something that looked like a generator and a case resembling a chest. Not just a generic, case but a very distinctive case. The case appeared to be made of lead and contained carvings on it. The carvings formed an ornate geometric pattern. Julian's knees buckled.

"These items are from what was the armory…."

Julian must have looked faint, because someone grabbed his arm to hold him up.

Argolan looked over and also reached out toward Julian while taking a step in his direction, "Are you all right?"

When Julian looked up he noticed that Argolan too was a little flushed. "I…." Julian struggle to catch his breath.

"Medical to the Ops Center," someone called out over the intercom.

But Julian put out his hand and shook his head. "I'm okay'" he managed to say.

"Catch your breath, son."

Julian took two deep breaths and exhaled them slowly.

"I…I've seen that case before!"

This caught everybody's attention, including Commander Young's.

"Are you sure?" asked Argolan. "Where?"

"I don't know where, but I am certain."

With that, Julian excused himself from the Ops Center with some resistance from Argolan who wanted him to go to the infirmary. He needed to go back to his quarters to pray and meditate. He would remember where he had seen that case before, but how long it would it take?

Chapter 8

Breakfast

It had been three days since Commander Young's transmission to Sharanda. Julian had spent almost all of that time in isolation praying and meditating, trying to remember where he had seen that case before, to no avail. Ever since Etty Prime, Julian's prayers usually yielded little, thus he expected little. Sometimes, however, the answer would sit on the edge of his consciousness, taunting him, like a shadow seen out of the corner of his eye. As soon as he turned to look at the shadow it would disappear without leaving a trace. Perhaps seeing the case in person would spark his memory. He would have that opportunity today as the ATS Focus was due to land this morning.

While he waited, Julian figured he would have breakfast. He called Argolan on intercom and asked if he would join him. Argolan agreed.

As Julian made his way to his and his father's favorite breakfast restaurant he had time to think. However, he didn't use this time to think about the box but rather, about his father. Commander Young would be arriving almost any minute with a cargo of what was inarguably the most momentous salvage operation in human history, bar none. This could quite possibly have an even more profound impact on the way mankind viewed itself than the archaeological discovery of the Garden of Eden. Even in these circumstances, as busy as he was with preparation, Argolan made time for Julian. He had always made time for him. Argolan hadn't just been a good father. He had been an exceptional father. There was no price that he wouldn't have paid for Julian or Faith.

When they were children, he had always been there to play with them, help them learn to ride a bicycle or read a book, or just look up at the night sky of Sharanda. Argolan had always been there for them, even when his wife died.

Argolan's wife (Faith's mother) had died very young. Julian was about seven years old, and he hadn't been with them very long, so he barely could remember her at all. Faith, being two years older than Julian, took it pretty hard. Nonetheless she had shielded Julian from it to some extent by taking him under her wing as a mother would. Of course they had played as all children do, but she was always there to take care of him when he was in need.

So was Argolan.

Julian had grown up to be very much like Argolan. He had such intense love and admiration for him that he would often guide his decisions by thinking about how Argolan would react in a given situation and then doing just that.

As Julian arrived at the One Star Diner he could see Argolan already sitting in "their booth" waiting for him.

"Did you get lost, son?" Argolan quipped. In reality Argolan's quarters were much closer to "The Star" than Julian's.

"Well, you have an age advantage over me," Julian shot back with a grin.

Trudy, the waitress, approached their table. "Hey, boys," she began, "How goes the Empire?"

"Imperial," Responded Argolan, "How's Gus? I haven't seen him the last couple of times I've been in."

"He's off today. Actually he's been working less and less, of late. I think he's getting about ready to sell the place. Hey, Argolan, you buy things for a living….."

Argolan put up his hand to stop her, "Only things of value."

Trudy feigned being taken aback with a gasp. "I'm going to tell him you said that. So what will it be, boys, the usual?"

Both men nodded, and off Trudy went to put through their orders.

Argolan turned to Julian with a grave look. "Julian, I believe the Guild may be making its move on the Trade Empire."

"After all of these years of leaving us alone, why would you think that?"

"Our deep scans have picked up a command ship and four warships just outside of our star system."

Julian pondered this information for a moment. "If the Guild wanted to take us down, wouldn't it just do so by creating constricting laws around our proverbial necks?"

"Only if it was willing to throw away the strength of the Trade Empire. You see, when someone profits, it is good for everybody. Because of what we have built here in the Galafon System, the New Territories are the wealthiest, most densely populated section of the Galaxy. The other star systems out here prosper because our business associates come here. When on their way here, or perhaps on their way out, they might stop at other worlds in the New Territories. Maybe they engage in commerce there. Maybe they vacation and sight-see there but either way, our business draws them to this area of the Galaxy.

"In addition our employees prosper here. They, in turn, go to these other worlds in the New Territories and engage in various activities. Next there's the Sigma System. Twenty-four worlds whose economies are completely fueled by trade as a direct result of our little Empire. Imagine those thousands of businesses with whom we supply goods going out of business because it becomes economically unfeasible to get supplies. While we employ relatively few people (on the scale of interstellar economics) do you know how many people those independent shops employ? Hundreds of millions. Those mass layoffs would not buy the Guild any favor out here. Either way, success is like a magnet, benefiting everybody in your vicinity. As a result the Galafon System, the Sigma System and in fact all of the systems in the New Territories, have flourished."

Argolan continued, "If the Guild went after us legally it would slow our prosperity. The Guild knows this. The center of influence which the

Empire now enjoys in the New Territories would begin to disintegrate, and it would no longer have any influence on these systems. However, if the Guild could take the Empire over without interrupting business too profoundly, then it could assume the Empire's great influence in the region. By seizing control of the largest economic infrastructure in the New Territories, the Guild would force all to bow to it lest trade be interrupted. That is a small but important part of why integrity is so fundamental to economics."

Julian thought again. "But four warships and one command ship would not be anywhere enough power to take us. They would need hundreds of times that amount of firepower."

"Oh, the Guild is not planning on having a single shot fire. That would interrupt production and lessen the leverage it would have over these other worlds. The Guild is going to attempt to put some sort of political pressure on us to 'voluntarily' allow it to assume the reigns."

"We can't let that happen, father. We're it. There is no more economic freedom in the Galaxy besides our institution. This is a bastion of hope for all who seek more out of life. This is it. We must protect it, with our lives if necessary."

Would he really protect it with his life, Julian wondered? He doubted it. Yet he wanted to believe he would.

Argolan's face lit up in a smile. "You have learned well, son. I am proud of you. You are ready to take over the Empire when I decide to let it go. I am very proud of you."

Argolan had always edified Julian, yet affirmations like this from his father still warmed his heart.

"The truth is that I don't know if I will have the courage to stand and be counted when the time comes." said Julian.

Argolan hunched toward Julian as if about to whisper a secret to him, but instead said very authoritatively, "Son, it is your purpose to lead the Empire into its next era of greatness."

"Why do you say that?"

"I just know. Call it the whisperings of The Spirit"

"But I'm weak!" Julian argued.

"You're strong. I've been telling you that your whole life. I see this strength in you, this…greatness. It far surpasses anything that I could ever hope to become. You need to understand that when you were young you suffered a tragedy the magnitude of which most will never know. It was an amazing burden to be put on such a young, innocent soul."

"But if it is my destiny to lead the Emp-"

"I said 'purpose,' not 'destiny.'" Argolan interrupted.

"What's the difference?"

"Destiny is something you are compelled to do, almost like being placed in a river with a swift current which continually washes you downstream whether you want to go there or not. The Lord places people in the Galaxy for a purpose. He calls us to serve. We can choose to answer that call or not. This is called 'agency,' the ability to choose. I know you will live up to your purpose, which is that of greatness."

At that moment their food came, which made Julian perfectly happy as he didn't know what to say. For the next few minutes both men ate without saying a word.

After finishing his breakfast Julian decided to prod Argolan for a little more information. "Father, with all that is going on how did you find time to meet with me this morning?"

"Son, you and Faith are the most important things in this Galaxy to me. I could hear that you needed to get some time alone with me by the tone in your voice when you called. I will always be there when you need me. Besides, we will not be unloading the Focus's cargo. You and I will inspect it on the ship, then the science team will do its studies there, after which we will determine its fate. We have never seen anything like this before, alien technology and all. The best science crew in our Empire is on the Focus, and it makes sense to me to have them do their studies in their home environment

"As far as the naval contingent is concerned, it won't be here for hours, and there really is nothing to be done about it now. Even if this is the beginning of our showdown with the Guild, which I suspect it is, Sharanda will not be ground zero in our war. The Guild is just setting things into motion. This is a chess match, and I think the Guild may be developing its queen too early. At this point we need to just sit back and observe. We'll counter when the time is right."

While Argolan was correct and the wheels of the Guild were turning in preparation to make its move on the Trade Empire, this was not the design of Masse's plans. If, in fact, Argolan had known it was Masse's command ship heading for Sharanda, he might have been able to thwart his plans, but this was not the case.

"When do we need to inspect the Focus's cache?" asked Julian

"Zero nine hundred hours."

"Great, that gives me time to see someone before. I'll meet you in the hanger."

Chapter 9

The Commerce of Sharanda

As Julian made his way through the maze of roads that comprised Empire City, he watched the commerce that was going on around him. Empire City, located deep inside of Mount Efil on Sharanda, was a world unto itself. There were kiosks, malls, arcades, war games, super markets, fruit stands and almost any other kind of small business imaginable. The fruit stands here were amazing. To understand the fruit industry that stemmed from Sharanda, one needs to understand the history of man's expansion across the Galaxy.

Although there have been doomsayers throughout Old Earth's history, Earth still remains completely hospitable to this day. There was never a nuclear war. No global warming other than that brought on by the natural cycles of any star system. There was never even a killer asteroid, earthquake, or volcano. In fact Old Earth is a veritable paradise to this day. Man left Old Earth because of nothing more than a pioneer spirit, the same pioneer spirit that drove the Europeans of the Fifteenth Century to explore the North American Continent, the same spirit which later drove the North American settlers to explore westward.

It began with the development of the light engine system. With this system a ship had a complex system of laser emitters on its stern. The emitters fired the lasers at specific points on the back of the ship where a highly sophisticated energy shield was located. The combination of the lasers and the shield created a physical interaction. This "pushed" the ship on the beams of light (almost as two magnets with the same pole in line would repel each other) enabling a body to travel at up to light speed in a straight line.

The speed the vessel moved could be altered by precise tuning of the shields. As a result of tuning, the shields allowed a certain portions of the light to pass through them as opposed to creating the push. Using extremely complex mathematical formulae, the push/pass-through ratio could be calculated. Cross referencing push/pass-through ratios with size, mass and, shape formulae for the ship which the engine was pushing enabled precise calculation of the speed at which the vessel would move. Thus the light engine was not really an engine at all, but more like a wave on which the ship rode.

However, the great breakthrough in the light engine system, the breakthrough which enabled interstellar travel, occurred when scientists discovered that by shooting a laser beam through a chamber containing a certain mixture of gases, the beam of light exited the chamber before it had traveled its length. The light beam traveled backward in time, arriving at its destination — outside of the far exterior of the chamber — before it had time to complete traveling the chamber's length. Placing this type of chamber on the stern of a ship, between its laser emitters and its shields, equipped the ship to ride on previous sequential beams of light and gave it the ability to move at almost infinite speeds.

After the creation of the advanced light engine, a probe was launched from Earth to explore nearby star systems. Over the next decade, many planets were discovered, which would possibly have been capable of supporting human life had the atmosphere been up to the task. In spite of the failure of these missions to discover a habitable planet, a groundswell of exploration enthusiasm ensued. This began a massive push on Old Earth to develop teraforming technology as was shown in science fiction movies of that era. Unfortunately, this technology never worked. In fact there were disasters that occurred in some of the attempts to teraform planets that killed tens of thousands of people and permanently poisoned some of these worlds. A faction arose on Old Earth, people who believed in the status quo. Eventually they were able to stop all of these projects by enacting laws that outlawed all teraforming science. But governments cannot easily crush the spirit of a true pioneer.

More probes utilizing the light engine system were built. Private corporations became involved. Science clubs and academies joined in. Before long, everyone seemed to have a stake in space exploration. Thousands of worlds were being explored in dozens of galaxies. And then it happened.

A private group of award-winning scientists had discovered a new star in the Milky Way Galaxy by sending out probes with highly specialized optical collectors. One of these probes picked up a star which was quickly named Opus. Not only was Opus home to *a* planet which could support human life, but, there were thirty-two planets capable of supporting man.

Once Opus was discovered, Mankind began a mad dash to create ships with light engines which were capable of transporting human beings there. Once there, it was a hop, skip and a jump to the Haron System which had three planets capable of supporting human life.

How does this relate to fruit? Had the Twentieth Century sci-fi vision of teraforming worlds come to fruition, man may not have had the drive to create the technology necessary to colonize deep space. Instead of discovering the unique environments of distant worlds and leaving them to their natural wonder, Man would have made them copies of Old Earth. All autochthonous vegetation would have given way to facsimiles of Old Earth's vegetation because the indigenous ecosystems would have been destroyed in favor of Earth-like ecosystems. Since teraforming nearby planets hadn't worked, man was forced to use his ingenuity to explore deep space. This led to the discovery of planets that, while being able to support human life, were still remarkably dissimilar to Old Earth, containing fresh, new ecosystems. Sharanda was one of those planets. If Sharanda could have been teraformed, it probably would have been in order to make it more hospitable.

To this day, Sharanda gives off a unique type of radiation. While that radiation has no effect on animal life, it profoundly affects vegetation.

The vegetation grows enormous. As a result, fruits and vegetables grown there also have an extraordinarily long period of perfect ripeness (sometimes years), and flavor like nothing else in the Galaxy. Julian observed the fruit merchants at work selling to their customers, many of whom came from other worlds to buy the fruit. Some of these traders would buy shiploads of merchandise and then sell it on their home worlds.

Fruit was not the only industry in Mount Efil. It was a complete city with roads, vehicles, hundreds of independent industries, a culture and a sense of community. More than fifty thousand families lived there, with a total of a little more than one hundred thirty thousand residents approximately one hundred thousand of whom were adults. Nearly eighty thousand of those adults worked for the Trade Empire. Almost all of the employees of the Trade Empire had entrepreneurial pursuits on the side, owning family businesses. Often the spouses and children of the Empire's employees ran these businesses. This was part of Argolan's genius. He took a useless world and built it into the epicenter of commerce in the Galaxy held together by a vested interest on the part of all who live there. Never had this been done at any other time or in any other place in the Galaxy.

As Julian approached the row of homes, he could already see Gabriel waiting for him outside on his front porch. Unlike Julian's neighborhood in which the living quarters were caverns with doors cut in rows directly into the stone face of Mount Efil, Gabriel's neighborhood was comprised of actual, free-standing homes. These homes were somewhat reminiscent of the brownstones built in Queens, New York, in the early part of the Twentieth Century back on Old Earth.

There was an irony here. On Old Earth, in the latter half of the Twentieth Century, organized crime had its seat of power in New York. Many of the families who led these organizations lived in the brownstones of Queens. Gabriel's father and mother had come to Sharanda from the Sigma System. They had come to Sharanda seeking refuge from their families who had run organized crime syndicates in the Sigma System. When they arrived there, they moved into the section of Mount Efil which most closely resembled the domiciles of the olden day organized crime families.

Julian reached Gabriel's porch, and Gabriel bounded down the steps and hugged Julian. "It's great to see you," he said. "What's been keeping you so busy? We usually get together within forty eight hours of being off-ship."

Julian brought him up to speed recounting his rest, his father's remarkable return from the near dead, the move of the Guild and the Focus's strike.

"It figures that old son of a gun would strike this load!" Gabriel said somewhat despondent. Gabriel was Julian's best friend and he knew (as did everyone within the hierarchy of the Trade Empire) that Julian needed to watch his back where Young was concerned.

"I don't mind that it was Young. There are many who would embrace my downfall." That statement was not really true, although Julian was so modest that he didn't really know it. Julian had earned the love and respect of all those who knew him. "What is troubling me is the chest." Julian explained this particular item and the feeling he had had since seeing it.

Gabriel had always been a sounding board for Julian. He was a truly good man and a trusted advisor. When it did become Julian's day to run the Empire, Gabriel would play a critical role in Imperial affairs. However, Julian had noticed that there had been somewhat of a shadow hanging over Gabriel's spirit of late. This had concerned him but he did not bring it up in their conversation. They talked for about a quarter of an hour, and Julian left to meet his purpose.

Chapter 10

ATS Focus

Argolan, Julian and Commander Young toured the cargo areas of the Focus which contained its finds. The Trade Federation had never made a score quite like this. Of course Julian was interested in only one of the items, something to which Young seemed entirely oblivious.

When he could contain himself no longer, Julian asked, "Commander Young, where is the chest?"

Young smiled. He had been anticipating this question. He was astounded that Mr. Paul had been able to keep his composure for as long as he had. He had been toying with him. Julian would inherit the empire which Young had helped Argolan to build. And why? For no better reason than Argolan had found him stranded on some third-rate mining world. This runt had essentially stolen Young's life work, and he had no mind to stand for it.

"We have the chest in a controlled area in the science laboratory. Our scientists, Abraham Kalman and Brian Schultz, have been performing a workup on it. I suppose you would like to see it?"

Julian could sense the venom coming from Young. Young seemed to feel as if Julian was stepping on his toes, but Julian had never understood why. "Yes, would that be possible?"

"Of course," Young replied with a huff. Even Argolan caught that. He looked toward Julian and gave a slight dismissive wave with his right hand as if to say, "Ignore him."

The Focus was the crown jewel of the Trade Empire. Aside from Argolan's original ship, the one with which he started the business, the Focus was the preeminent ship of the Trade Empire's fleet. It was the first ship representing the expansion of the Empire beyond Argolan himself. It was it plush, with wall-to-wall carpeting everywhere. Sitting areas with bookshelves containing antique books were ornamented by luxurious couches. The wall rails were padded. Elevators moved vertically from deck to deck. Artwork adorned the walls everywhere. The Focus also contained every sort of recreation area possible. It symbolized, as well as optimized, the success of the Trade Empire.

In contrast, the Liahona was little more than a tin can with a light engine. It was safe, but there were no creature comforts. This didn't bother Julian. As he figured it, Young had worked very hard most of life to help build the Empire. He had been a beacon of integrity in all of his dealings with and for Argolan. He had earned this trophy.

As the company entered the science lab Julian could see Schultz and Kalman working away in the controlled area.

There it sat directly in front of them. The chest.

It was small, perhaps one foot deep, eighteen inches wide and eight inches high. Its exterior was almost boastful, containing ornate etchings on the top and sides. Julian imagined that whatever it contained was highly prized.

Kalman worked from within the controlled area while wearing a protective suit. He took notice of the approaching group and stopped performing the scans he had been running of the container. He pressed a button on his suit and spoke to Young via the intercom. "Commander," he said "we know how to open it."

Young went to the intercom on the console next to him and queried, "Any risk of contamination?"

"Cannot be determined. This container is made from the same material as the derelict's airlock door. Scans can't penetrate. I would like permission to open it in the controlled area."

Young looked toward Argolan, who being careful not to step on his friend's toes on his own ship, just smiled.

"Permission granted, Abraham. Please be careful."

Julian couldn't believe what he witnessed. Some kind of liquid was applied to the surface of the hinges on the box. Then a cold laser was applied to the liquid, and the hinges shattered away. He had never seen anything like it before.

Kalman went back to his console and programmed shield metrics into it. A flat shield, approximately sixteen feet deep by two feet wide, with a plane parallel to the ground, materialized approximately ten inches above the floor. It hovered in front of the chest. Kalman inputted some more metrics, and the shield moved toward the chest. It slid into the chest, between the body of the container and the lid, the way a bookmark could be slipped between the pages of a closed book. Once it was fully inserted so there was a perimeter of shield protruding from all four sides of the chest, Kalman entered additional information into his work station. This time, the shield lifted straight up toward the ceiling, lifting the chest's lid until it hovered about four feet above the chest.

Kalman hit several buttons on his workstation and reported, "No signs of danger. No contaminants or explosives detected. There is, however, a faint energy signature being detected, but I read no moving parts."

Kalman pushed yet another sequence of buttons and grabbed a joystick that was protruding from his work station. Down came a camera from a structure in the top of the controlled area. As the camera gently descended, Julian tingled with anticipation. He must have given away his enthusiasm because Argolan looked over at him and smiled. Julian smiled back. They had always had such a strong bond. Every day since finding him, Argolan had worked feverishly to strengthen that bond.

While Kalman could see the transmission from the camera no one else could. "This is interesting. Inside the box is a triangular item. It is suspended in the case in mid-air as if held there by a force field, except that I am not reading any kind of a force field energy signature. The triangle is emanating a faint light."

With that, Kalman buried his head back into his work station. Other tools descended from the ceiling into the box.

"Father, I would like to see it," Julian said.

"Lawrence," Argolan said gently to Young.

Young huffed while he pushed the intercom button. To think he had to play the part of a trained orangutan for that insufferable brat.

"Abraham, do you think it would be safe to use an energy grappler to remove the item from its case?"

"I can detect no traps or other dangers. It should be fine," Kalman answered as he resumed working at his station.

Suddenly a shield exactly in the shape of a human's right hand appeared in the middle of the controlled area. Next Kalman pushed a sequence of buttons on his workstation, and a hologram of the chest appeared on the floor about five feet in front of him.

Kalman pushed a button on his work station and a force field engulfed his left arm. He then proceeded to remove the right glove from his protective suit, grabbed a glove from his work station and put it on his right hand. As Kalman did so the energy grappler leaped to about five feet in front of the real chest to correspond with Kalman's proximity to the holographic chest. When Kalman finished locking the replacement glove onto the cuff of his suit he terminated the force field which had protected him during the exchange of gloves and began to walk toward the holographic chest. As he maneuvered, the energy grappler made corresponding movements toward the real chest. It was a sight to watch the grappler move, just dangling and moving back and forth, like the hand of a person who was walking. However, the person could not be seen.

As Kalman approached the holograph he knelt. Once positioned, he reached into the holographic representation of the chest and grabbed the holographic triangle. At the same time the energy grappler reached into the real chest and extracted its contents. It was eerie to watch the real hand grab the virtual object, while at the same time, the force field hand aped the action exactly and grabbed the real object. "Kind of ironic," Julian thought.

Kalman held forth the object for all to see. It was triangular. It appeared to be an equilateral triangle. Each side was approximately ten inches long with a ribbon etched into the middle of each side. On each side above and below the ribbon, a soft glow radiated which extended to about an inch from the corners.

Mesmerized, the company approached the shield.

"Commander," Julian asked, "May we take a closer look?"

Young scowled while he hit the intercom. "Abraham, could we drop the shield?"

Kalman went back to his work station. As he did, the grappler imitated his every move with mechanical precision.

After a few more minutes of scanning, Kalman approved the action. Kalman hit a button, and a computer voice came over the intercom in the science lab. "Ninety seconds until containment release. Sixty seconds until containment release. Thirty seconds until containment release. Fifteen seconds until containment release. Ten, nine, eight, seven, six, five, four, three, two, one. Containment release engaged."

With that the containment field flickered and then disappeared. Time seemed to stop. And then…

Chapter 11

The Device

The device began to glow intensely. Suddenly, all in the room felt a single momentary pulse run through them. It gently lifted Julian about an inch off of the floor. The sensation reminded Julian of being in the ocean up to his shoulders when a wave came and gently lifted him slightly off of the sea floor.

All at once, everything in the room that wasn't attached to some structure shifted slightly. The lights began to flicker. The electric grappler disappeared and the object fell freely to the floor.

Argolan looked at Julian. "Did everyone else sense that?"

Everyone reported affirmatively.

Argolan ran to the intercom. "Ops Center, report!"

A voice which Julian couldn't place responded, "We can't explain it, sir. Everything sort of just…….shifted. Now we are experiencing some technical disruptions."

"I'll be right there." Argolan responded.

Argolan turned to Young and in his authoritative voice said, "Commander, put your full science team on this. Figure out what just happened. I want everything, everything with any writing or symbols such as the chest and the key pad to be sent to the Cryptography and Intelligence Center. They are to interpret all of it as expeditiously as possible. Have your science team work non-stop to figure out what that device is and what it just did. Have I made myself clear?"

"Yes, sir." Young responded.

Chapter 12

Status Report

The Operations Center was not more than a couple of miles from the hanger but it was a tough couple of miles. Buried deep in the bowels of Mount Efil, the Ops Center was at the end of a huge labyrinth of corridors which had been cut into the mountain. When Mount Efil was made into the base for the Trade Empire, the actual excavation, while expansive (it took thousands of laborers almost five years to tunnel it out) was not the most difficult part of building the facility.

Argolan knew that there would be challenges with having people live inside all of the time. Humans could go outside on Sharanda. Although it was capable of supporting human life, it was inhospitable. It was a desert, there was water but almost none on the surface and constant wind blew, endlessly shifting the sand. The inherent challenges of living inside could only be combated by making the indoors feel like the outdoors. This would require, among other things, that specific lighting techniques be used to offer the feel of genuine sunlight. This was the most difficult part of building the facility. Every little corridor had to be perfectly lighted, and getting it just right had been a massive undertaking in the scopes of engineering and labor.

As Argolan and Julian made their way through the maze of corridors leading from the hanger down to the Ops Center, Julian was deep in thought. Argolan picked up on this. He had the gift of being able to read people clearly. "Son, share your thoughts with me." Julian stopped walking. He didn't know where to begin.

"Come, we must be expeditious in our return to the Ops Center," Argolan urged.

They resumed walking.

"Well, first I have seen that case before, and I can't put my finger on where. It's driving me crazy. I know I've seen it, but that is an impossibility! Next, why did you send those items to the Cryptography and Intelligence Center instead of to the Linguistics Institute? I assume you hope to glean some information from the writing and symbols on those items."

They reached the Ops Center and Argolan stopped outside of the door. He decided that this teaching moment with his son was worth one minute.

"Son, you will remember where you have seen the chest before. As far as the Intelligence Center is concerned, the experts there are the right people for this job. The Linguistics Foundation is here to help us communicate with other humans. Every language spoken by humans on the more than two thousand inhabited planets in the Galaxy is a derivative of some language that was spoken on Old Earth. That gives the Institute a base from which to start. In this instance, however, the linguists will almost certainly not be able to start from that foundation. This is more along the lines of cracking a cryptogram. When dealing with a cipher, the creator of the code attempts to offer as little a basis from which to start unlocking it as possible. In other words, a code based in English would be easier for me to decipher than a code based in a language with which I am unfamiliar. So while the Institute would not have its normal basis with which to start deciphering the symbols, that is exactly what the Cryptography and Intelligence Center does. They decipher things with an obscured, unknown, or hidden basis. This is precisely a job for them."

As always Julian was in awe of Argolan's wisdom. How would he ever be able to fill this man's shoes?

With that Argolan put his palm up in front of the DNA reader which was to the left of the door and it scanned him. The Ops Center door slid open. As soon as they entered the room Argolan was off and running. "Marco, what is our status?"

"Sensors are off line. Electrical problems are being reported en mass. Reports of a 'shift' are pouring in from all over Mount Efil. And believe it or not, we have had a couple of reports of this nature from our ships out in space," was the reply of Marco Toms. While Toms was the assistant director of operations, he manned the communications console in the absence of his boss, Gayle Chase.

Argolan gasped in disbelief. "In space?"

"Yes, but all such reports have originated from relatively close proximity to the Sharanda."

"Relatively close proximity to Sharanda. What precisely does that mean?" Argolan was clearly a touch aggravated by the obvious lack of understanding displayed by Toms. He continued, "We just had a device the size of a book without any discernable power source generate a pulse which effected our ships in space. They are what, two million miles away? Three million? That may be close if you're talking about making a jump with a light drive, but in this instance I wouldn't say that's close. I......"

"Excuse me," Deirdre Lane, the Empire's communications director, interrupted, "I just received a report from the Mustang that they just experienced it too."

"Dear Lord, the Mustang is more than six light months from here. How far can the effect have extended?" asked Toms rhetorically.

"Excuse me again, Argolan," Lane said with urgency in her voice. "We have an incoming coded military communication. What shall I do?"

Julian felt deflated. "Wonderful, just as we're blinded, the vultures of the Guild arrive."

"Can you put it on screen?"

"I don't know, Argolan. I'll try."

Lane fidgeted for a few moments with the knobs, dials and sliders on her communications panel until an image appeared on the view screen. It was distorted at first, but Lane persisted. As she did, the image cleared up, until all of a sudden it was crystal clear. Julian looked at Argolan and could tell that clearly the image didn't please him. His mouth was agape.

"Masse!"

"Argolan, what the hell have you done to us?" was the angered response.

"As you can see Admiral we have taken a hit, too. In fact, we have reports pouring in from our ships all over the Galaxy that they have experienced the same difficulties that you and I are currently experiencing.

"Hold," Masse said and the screen went black.

Julian turned to Argolan, "Is he planning his attack?"

"Doubtful. They are even more confused than we are. I did not see this coming. I do not think that the Guild would have sent Masse to make its move. They would have to have expected outright defiance from me based on our history together."

Their history together was, at the least, interesting. Almost forty years ago, when Argolan had first started his salvage business and had only one ship, Masse was his second in command. They had been best friends for years. Argolan had always been the more ambitious of the two, but he had desperately wanted to bring Masse along on his journey to success, so he gave Masse a five percent stake in the operation and off they went. Of course when Masse signed on he brought his girlfriend, Angel, with whom he had been for over five years. Argolan had never cared much for her, but she was an engineer and as free labor was all he could afford at the time, an engineer would be an excellent asset in his new endeavor.

After getting to know her, Argolan revised his earlier opinion, finding Angel to be captivating. She was brilliant and attractive, yet she had a softness about her that made him want to hold her as a child would a kitten. Of course out of loyalty to Masse, Argolan wouldn't give his feelings any real consideration.

One day, while returning home after being out on a particularly long operation, using the little skiff from which they operated their business, Masse and Angel started to argue. What it was about Argolan no longer remembered. All he could remember was that Masse became angrier than he had ever seen him. He completely lost control. Masse's rage built until he finally struck Angel. This was completely unacceptable to Argolan. He grabbed Masse from behind around the shoulders, trying to restrain him. Somehow Masse broke free and spun around with a fist which caught Argolan across the cheek.

Argolan had stumbled backward a few steps, dazed. He must have blacked out for a moment because suddenly he found himself on the deck (floor) of the ship. When he came to, he could see Masse hunched over Angel, who was on her back on the floor. He was strangling her. Argolan got up, shook himself, removed his knife from his utility belt and plunged it into Masse's back.

Masse collapsed onto the deck. After Argolan helped Angel up they bound Masse, attempted to stop the bleeding from his wound and locked him in a utility closet. Argolan diverted the skiff's course to the nearest medical facility. They dropped the now-unconscious Masse off and left. Argolan and Angel thought that Masse had likely died in the medical facility, so they never gave him a second thought.

Shortly after Argolan and Angel married. Soon they had Faith, and seven years later took in a young child whose parents had been killed. Argolan had a blissful life. He had a wife with whom he was madly in love, two wonderful children who were the lights of his life and a rapidly growing business which had just moved its base of operations to Sharanda.

Then came the accident. Argolan and Angel were working on a ship that was the casualty of a pirate attack, when Angel became a little careless, and tripped a mine which the pirates had left behind. There was no explosion. The mine simply released an acid onto the deck of this single-level vessel. It ate a hole through the hull, and Angel was pulled out into space. Thankfully, she was the only one in the compartment, and the suction of the ship's air escaping into the great vacuum of space pulled the door shut, sparing the rest of the crew.

The funeral was difficult. Faith was hurt and angry and Argolan didn't know how he was going to go on. Then a young Guild bureaucratic officer walked into the service. He had a familiar look, but Argolan couldn't place him. He looked old and tired for his years, wearing the Guild uniform of submission.

As the service ended mourners came to Argolan to offer their condolences. Argolan could see the officer waiting patiently at the back of the line. The line moved slowly until finally the officer was face to face with Argolan. The officer said nothing but just stared into Argolan's eyes icily.

Finally Argolan couldn't take it anymore. "Do I know you?"

"You don't recognize me!"

Argolan knew that deep, husky voice.

"Masse! We thought...."

"That you had killed me? You did. I lost everything that day. You forgot all about it, but I didn't. I have thought about it every single day for the past ten years. The only hope I held was that one day you would meet with an untimely demise, and I would be able to get my Angel back. Now you have killed her, too."

Argolan didn't know what to say. He simply stood speechless and unmoving.

Masse moved closer, positioning his mouth over Argolan's left shoulder and whispered, "I promise that you will meet with that untimely demise, but first, I am going to hurt you until you can't feel anymore."

With that Masse turned and walked away. Most people would have found this to be disturbing, but not Argolan. An hour earlier he had felt as though he lost everything on that ship and didn't know how he would carry on. However, after seeing him, Argolan realized that Masse was a man who had lost everything. He had allowed bitterness to consume him. Argolan vowed to himself that in spite of Angel's death he would not let that happen to him.

Over the years, as Masse joined and then rose to great acclaim in the military, he accumulated more power and influence in the Galaxy. During that time he had pretty much just harassed Argolan and the Trade Empire. However, he had simply been biding his time. For more than thirty years this wound had festered, and now it was time to purge the infection.

The view screen came back to life showing Masse's face. "Open a corridor to receive my party."

"Hold," Argolan said. He turned to Naziz Kumar, the Empire's director of security, and said, "Naziz, I want a squad of armed security officers outside the hangar bay's south and east entrances. I want an open communications line piped from me to each squad. I don't want them to be seen. If Masse forces us to move from the hangar, I will give the teams verbal cues as we begin to move. I will want the team in front of us to drop back just out of sight, and the team behind us to follow just out of sight. I'll let them know if we need them to move in. I also want a third team to meet us at the hangar. They should only carry sidearms which will stay holstered. They will come into the hangar with us. Am I clear?"

"Yes, Argolan," Kumar responded.

"Screen on."

"What do you think you're doing, putting me on hold?" Masse snapped.

"I just needed to work out some logistics. You're cleared to land. Your window will open in T minus three minutes. Corridor Beta. Argolan out."

The screen went dead.

"Come, Julian."

Chapter 13

A Loud Meeting

Julian and Argolan watched the hangar bay doors open to reveal the hidden landing corridor. They were ready. A squad of fifteen security officers with holstered sidearms waited along side them for the landing of the Soulseeker. The Soulseeker was Masse's personal shuttle. He had aptly named it, swearing to take away Argolan's soul and life. Of course the true reason for the name was something Masse kept to himself.

As the Soulseeker landed, chills rippled down Julian's spine. There was something about Masse that made Julian uneasy; anxious. They had had a few minor encounters over the years. Julian also knew that there was bad blood between Masse and his father but didn't know the details. Whatever had happened between the two had caused Argolan great pain, and he didn't like to discuss it. Argolan would have been happier to simply avoid Masse all together. Masse was another story, as he often harassed the Trade Empire. Julian didn't know exactly why. All he knew was that he had looked into Masse's eyes many times, and all he could see was the fire of hatred burning in his soul. It reminded Julian of the dagger that stuck in his own side.

Coward. You will run from anything.

Julian felt safe, however, with his father there.

Once the Soulseeker touched down, its four landing feet retracted setting its belly on the flight deck. The ground-level hatch opened, and out walked Masse followed by an odd-looking officer with an appearance more like that of a bureaucrat than a soldier. Twenty-five heavily armed Navy SEALs with laser rifles drawn accompanied them.

The SEALs were the killing machines of the Galactic Navy's forces, feared and respected across the Galaxy. During the Galactic Wars, these sailors had single-handedly defended Old Earth, the Galactic capital planet, from attack while vastly outnumbered. They were honorable heroes who had the respect of all Mankind. However, as with everything he touched, Masse had corrupted the SEALs in his fleet, and they were now little more than killer sheep. Then again, even if it were not for Masse, the upper echelons of the military's command had long ago fallen to Guild loyalty. On its own, that would have corrupted the entire Navy.

Without acknowledging anyone else, Masse walked directly to Argolan and, facing him nose-to-nose, growled, "We need to talk. In private."

"We can take the south exit and go to the south auxiliary room." This was the only cue that the team outside of the south exit needed to begin to drop back.

"I don't need the cartography lessons. Let's just go. Your goons stay here."

"Is he planning to kill me?" This was the first thought which ran through Argolan's mind. If he did it would be the last thing Masse ever did as there would be a squadron of security guards in the southern corridor leading away from the auxiliary room. As Argolan took his first step to begin leading Masse to the auxiliary room, a hand reached out and grabbed his arm. It was Julian.

"Father, do not go with him."

"It will be fine. You wait here with the men." Argolan feigned calmness, but he was visibly scared.

"No. I will not let him lead you off to the slaughter like a la…."

"Shut up," Masse commanded Julian, taking two steps toward him. "Do you think that you are in control here? Whether he lives or dies is up to me alone. Is that clear?!" It was more of an order than a question.

Coward! The dagger twisted in Julian's side as he shrunk back from Masse.

This man, Argolan, meant everything to Julian. Was he going to allow it to end like this? Like he did with his parents? Julian was frozen.

Coward!

Masse looked at Julian in disgust. A slight smirk came across his face. "He knows I am a coward," Julian thought.

"Fine, accompany us." Masse finally said.

Julian shuddered as he and Argolan began to move toward the south entrance.

"Wait!" Masse barked. "Remove your sidearms and Argolan, remove that utility belt. I have not forgotten your blade's bite." One of the SEALs took their equipment.

"You stay here!" Masse barked at the SEALs while signaling with his hands, signals Julian couldn't make out. Masse pointed at the soldier who resembled a bureaucrat, and said, "Donahue, come with us."

Donahue spoke for the first time.. "Sir, don't you think that some of our escort should accompany us?" Julian could tell that he was clearly scared by Masse, although he hid it well. One coward can always sense another.

Rage boiled within Masse. He quickly walked over to Donahue. Then, even though Julian had caught a glimpse of the monster deep within Masse's soul, Masse's next move stunned him.

Masse extended his right hand and gripped Donahue's throat.

"I have had about enough of your questioning my orders. Don't push me......."

Masse sort of dragged the word 'me' out. Julian could see the man trying to contain the monster. It was like a coiled serpent about to strike its prey.

"We move now!" Masse barked.

The group began to move toward the auxiliary room with Julian and Argolan leading the way, Masse and Donahue following behind. Argolan silently cursed himself for allowing his son to get caught up in his fight. If anything happened to Julian he would never be able to forgive himself.

"How much farther?" an aggressive voice asked from the rear.

Argolan replied, "It's that room straight ahead of us."

"Stop here," Masse barked, pulling a gun from his utility belt. Argolan stepped between Masse and Julian. Masse chuckled at the old fool. He walked to the right wall of the narrow corridor and placed the barrel of the gun against the wall a couple of feet up from the floor. He pulled the trigger; there was a thud. He repeated the same action about four feet higher and then repeated the entire sequence on the wall to the left.

"Move!" Masse ordered.

They entered the auxiliary room.

Chapter 14

An Accosting, a Murder, A Kidnapping and a Slaughter

The auxiliary room contained a table with chairs and a computer terminal. Masse motioned to the chairs at the head of the table, and Julian and Argolan sat down. Donahue remained in the corner standing at the door while Masse sat across from the father-son team.

Slowly and deliberately, Masse reached his right hand into his jacket's left breast pocket. Every move that Masse made sent fear into Julian's heart. He was obviously unstable. Who knew when the man would no longer be able to control the serpent within?

Masse withdrew a group of rolled-up papers which were held closed by a rubber band. As he removed the rubber band, Julian could see that Masse was relishing every moment.

When he could no longer contain himself Masse smiled and said, "After all of these years I finally have you, Argolan!" With that he slid the now-unrolled papers across the table.

Argolan picked the papers up and began looking through them. The papers were a Sigman Commerce Bureau report documenting an unlicensed, illegal salvage operation by the ATS Liahona of a Ranasian warship left dead on a planet in the Ranis System. The war between Ranis and Embuieck had left many good caches for salvage. However, the Trade Federation always did everything legally. Nevertheless, here was the proof in his hands. The document had pictures of the Liahona and even of its crew in the act of harvesting the site.

The Trade Federation always went to such lengths to make certain everything was done legally. More than fifteen years ago, when she first recognized the Guild threat, Faith realized that the Trade Empire would need to become expert at using the law to shield itself from the law. She took it upon herself to become schooled in all aspects of law, meticulously studying all the restrictions which the Guild and courts placed on the salvage industry. She developed the Imperial Legal Alliance, an independent organization within the Trade Federation comprised of lawyers, legal and contract analysts and proprietary license obtainment experts who scrutinized salvage law and guidelines to determine which licenses and protocols were necessary for any given activity in any given place at any given time. All these groups were necessary evils due to the red tape and regulation of salvage laws. Was it possible that the Alliance's teams had overlooked something on this job? Argolan had a sinking feeling. Everything he had worked for during his adult life appeared about to fall apart.

Argolan looked up at Masse, who almost looked like a child on Christmas morning. "What do you want from me?"

"I want you to suffer," Masse said matter-of-factly. "I want your family to suffer. I want your Empire to crumble. I want all that is yours which should have been mine to become nothing more than a memory to you. I want to see the pain in your face. I want to see you crushed. Then, and only then, will I kill you, just like you did me all of those years ago."

With that, Donahue began shifting. Julian could clearly see Donahue was starting to understand that Masse's desire for the future of the Empire did not align with Donahue's. What could not be readily discerned by Julian was that Donahue was a Republic loyalist, Masse was not.

"Jim, YOU threw that away all on your own with your inability to control your temper. When YOU were placed under pressure YOU treated Angel like a toy with which you had grown tired of playing."

Masse grunted and slapped Argolan across the face with the back of his left hand. Argolan's head jerked to his right, but he didn't make a sound. Julian rose as if to attempt to move on Masse, but Masse was quick. He stepped back and instantly had his laser pistol aimed at Julian's head.

Donahue could not stay out of this any longer. Obviously Masse had lied to him about his "mission." Clearly Masse was not here at the orders of Naval Command, and yet he had allowed himself to become one of the key players in Masse's quest for revenge. He should have known. The challenge was Masse was such an adept liar that he could say almost anything and make it sound plausible. He was so charismatic that one wanted to believe him. Unfortunately, one couldn't.

Donahue stepped forward. "Admiral, I thin.."

Masse turned his laser pistol on Donahue. "You will get back into your corner, Captain. NOW!"

The unarmed Donahue shrank back. Argolan shook off the stunned feeling from having been assaulted and urged Julian to sit once again. He then turned his attention back to the document.

Argolan looked it over for content. He examined both sides of the document. It wasn't until he held it up to the light that he caught Masse's simple error which should never have been overlooked. Masse erred in presenting Argolan with the original report and not a copy. Until this moment Argolan thought that it was over for the Empire, that he would be forced to cede control over to Masse and that perhaps there was some legitimate legal boundary that the Trade Federation's legal department had overlooked on the Ranis job. Yes it was true that the Guild had left salvage relatively free to enterprise, but that was only relative to the fiasco that it had created in other industries. There were still many pitfalls one could step in if not careful. Then, poof, an Empire would crumble. But this wasn't the case today.

"Masse, these documents are forged."

Masse's smile disappeared for just a moment, Julian noted. Obviously Masse had not acquired the documents legitimately or this tiny doubt would never have been allowed into his consciousness. The smile returned.

"What are you trying to pull, Argolan?"

Of course Masse thought the documents were real. He had been dealing with his connection on Sigma, Zahn, who sold him these documents, for so long that he had grown to trust him. This time, however, Zahn had decided to betray Masse. This time the prize had been too good. The Trade Empire was clean, but there was a buyer for dirt on it. This time Zahn knew that Masse was so far over the line that he would have no recourse if he were to manufacture the evidence that Masse wanted to see. This time Zahn could sense the emotions in Masse were so strong that Masse would believe him just because he wanted to. This time would be the last time that Zahn would deal with Masse, and he accepted that. Of all the times Masse had dealt with Zahn, this was the worst possible time to have been betrayed. Masse had gone way out on a limb, and Zahn had sawed through the trunk of the tree from which he hung.

"The paper," was Argolan's response.

"The paper?" was Masse's incredulous response.

"Yes, look." Argolan held the document up toward the light. "This paper is not the paper on which the Sigman Commerce Bureau prints its documents.

Masse snickered. "So now you're an expert on the subject of paper?"

"I know because about fifteen years ago we did a salvage operation for the Commerce Bureau which involved a freighter load of their stock paper which had been commandeered by pirates. Do you see how light comes through the paper when I hold it up to the lights? Paper made from a special kind of tree called the Plumar, which solely grows on Sigma 11, is the only stock used to print government documents in that system. There is a certain nutrient in the earth on Sigma 11 which causes a buildup of a unique enzyme in the pulp of those trees. This phenomenon results in the prevention of all translucency of the wood of the Plumar tree, or in this instance, the paper made from the wood of this tree. If this document was printed on legitimate Commerce

Bureau stock, no light would pass through it. Of course, this is classified information." In spite of his fear, Argolan began to chuckle from the irony adding, "Kept secret to prevent forgery, actually."

Even Julian had to smile.

The Serpent was not smiling. The reality suddenly hit him that everything for which he had worked all of these years was gone in an instant. His credibility, his leverage, all of it. Because of that rodent Zahn. Masse had overplayed his hand because of Zahn's promises, and now he was exposed.

He was now completely beyond rational thought. In truth, he had lost this capacity along with his sanity many years ago. The monster gnawed at him. The betrayal of his best friend and the love of his life. His entire military career had been the means to accrue the power to destroy Argolan. And now, as his day to finally see that goal to fruition was here, it was slipping away from him.

"You!" Masse seethed. He yearned to kill Argolan. But he somehow controlled that urge. Instead Masse swung his laser pistol at Argolan's head with the full force of his right hand. When the handle of the pistol connected with Argolan's skull it made a sickening tearing noise. Argolan collapsed, his blood cascading across the floor.

Donahue had unwisely regained his courage. "What do you think you're doing?"

With that, Masse pointed his pistol at Donahue and squeezed the trigger. The nauseating smell of burning flesh filled the room. The sound from the discharge of the weapon alerted the security force waiting just outside the south entrance of the room.

As the south door started to open Masse grabbed Julian and held him tightly to his chest using him as a shield. Masse's left arm was around Julian's neck as they faced the south door, while his right hand held his pistol to Julian's right temple. Masse walked backward toward the north door. As the first of the security men stepped into the room, Masse tensed to show them that he meant business.

"Stop there or I'll kill him!" Masse declared. The security men stopped. Masse continued to urge Julian backward toward the door until he heard it open behind them. The two men stepped backward through the door.

Once through the door Masse released Julian. Pointing his gun at him he said, "Head back to the hanger." With Masse following, Julian walked briskly for a distance until Masse barked, "Stop."

Julian stopped and turned to face Masse. He watched as Masse pushed a red button on his black leather utility belt. The spikes that Masse had planted in the walls on the way to the Conference Room exploded, causing the hallway to cave in on itself, leaving it impassable.

"Continue," Masse barked, waving his gun toward the hangar.

They were in a flat out run as they got back to the hangar. A battle was raging there between the Navy SEALs that Masse had brought and the security squad that had been in the hangar with Argolan. The north entrance had been demolished. Julian figured that the hand signals Masse had given his men before leaving had instructed them to destroy that entrance to prevent other security regiments from entering.

Laser fire was everywhere. Each laser shot created a corresponding explosion at its point of impact. Masse grabbed Julian again to use as a shield. As they entered the hangar, the fire from the Empire Security Forces stopped. Masse continued until he was in the center of the room. Holding his gun to Julian's head, Masse yelled, "Put your weapons down and come to the center of the hangar."

There was no response.

"You have until I count to three, and then I will kill him."

There was shuffling behind some of the containers. "Okay," someone shouted. "Don't hurt him."

Julian couldn't take this. He had to do something, as he knew Masse would kill them if they disarmed. *Coward. You won't stop it.* But he had to. He couldn't let his friends be slaughtered by the Serpent. "Don't!" He yelled. "He'll kill you! He'll kill you!"

Men stepped out of some of the hangar bay's various nooks in they had been hiding. Once exposed, they dropped their guns and shuffled toward the center of the room.

Julian's pleas persisted, but the men did not take heed. They continued to walk forward. To Julian, it seemed to happen in slow motion. He continued to beg, to plead, as his friends forfeited their lives that his might be spared.

Masse's men moved forward, weapons trained on their prey. When the men reached the center of the hangar Masse gave Julian to one of the SEALs to hold and then approached the security officers.

Masse looked at the weakest of them. He pulled his hulking mass up to its full glory and demanded, "Is this everyone?"

The security officer, who was dwarfed by Masse's enormous frame, shrank back and replied, "Yes," with a shudder in his voice.

Masse turned around. His back was to the security officers for the first time. He collected Julian and walked toward the docking port of the Soulseeker. As he and Julian reached the ship Masse stopped. Without turning around he said, "Kill them."

Tears began to stream down Julian's face as the SEALs' blasters sang their deadly tune.

Chapter 15

Escape

As the Soulseeker lifted off, Masse expected a fight. None came. "Captain Rydell, signal Trade Empire Command. Send a message that our business here has concluded and request the corridor window be opened for our departure."

Julian sat next to him with his hands bound behind his back by force field binders. *Coward.* The dagger twisted. *You let your men, your friends die.* It was true. He should have done something to prevent their termination.

"Admiral," Rydell said, "We have been granted clearance."

Masse had fully expected the need to leverage Julian Paul's life in order to get their window opened. Something was wrong.

"Good, Captain. Signal the command ship to meet us as soon as we clear the corridor and have our warships standing at alert. Things didn't go quite as expected on Sharanda, we lost Donahue. Contact the Deference and order Parsons to meet us on the command ship" Masse glanced at Julian, who was staring off into space.

The trip through the window took approximately seven minutes. And true to plan, the command ship was there. The shuttle approached the command ship's landing bay, and Masse knew something was wrong. The exodus had been too easy.

The ship landed, the hatch opened, and all but two of the SEALs exited, those two stayed behind to act as an armed escort for Julian and

Masse. Masse stood up while one SEAL grabbed each of Julian's arms prompting him toward the exit. The SEALs brought him out of the ship but stopped him in the landing bay. As per orders, Steven Parsons, Donahue's executive officer, was awaiting them in the landing bay.

"Take him to my quarters and keep him under lock and key," Masse instructed his men. Off they dragged Julian, who had not so much as acknowledged the existence of anyone else since the horrific incident in the hangar on Sharanda. Masse turned, heading for the bridge.

Parsons approached Masse and inquired, "Sir, is Captain Donahue still on board the Soulseeker?"

"I am afraid that he was killed on Sharanda."

Parsons looked directly at Masse. The meeting of their eyes gave Parsons a chill he would never forget. It is said that the eyes are the window to the soul. Parsons noted that if this were true, Masse had no soul.

It was true, Masse had lost his soul, years earlier, as he had seethed over Argolan's perfidy every minute of every day for years. The pain of the (perceived) betrayal had been so acute that it consumed him. He couldn't eat or sleep. The only hope he'd held was that one day, after the acute memory of that fateful day's events softened, he would be able to reconcile with Angel.

Finally, years later, while still biding his time working for the Guild as a clerk, a communiqué was sent out over the system with Angel's death announcement. Masse's sole reason for going on was lost. This was Argolan's fault. Argolan had betrayed him to steal Angel for himself. All Masse thought about from that day forward was how to make Argolan pay for his betrayal. He became incapable of feeling anything other than the rage, the hatred and the anger. The monster was born within him. He had thrived on that anger for more than thirty years now.

As Argolan grew their (yes, their, his and Masse's) business, it became evident that he was becoming untouchable. Masse would need leverage to take Argolan down. The military would offer Masse the leverage he would need to take Argolan down. A command of his own would offer him that strength if manipulated properly.

Working for the Guild, Masse had begun to understand the inner workings of the military. It had atrophied under the (unofficial) control of the Guild. It had become political and bureaucratic. But that was good for Masse. He knew people. Being a clerk, he was the gatekeeper for the information flow to several of the most influential people in the Galaxy. He had spent the past few years cultivating relationships with these resources as well as learning many of their "dirty little secrets." Now it was time to utilize them. Weak groups are always susceptible to the influence of a strong leader, which Masse was. With those two things in mind he knew he would be able to develop clout quickly, clout which he could one day use to his own ends.

As a result of his drive, a drive which was fueled by the monster within, and his connections, he had ascended in the Navy very quickly. There had been times over the years when he had had opportunities to confront Argolan, but he had restrained himself. He had pestered the Empire over the years to be sure, but it wasn't until the day that Zahn had made contact with him about the incriminating "evidence" that he had decided to make his move. Unfortunately that worm Zahn had betrayed him by selling him a forged document. Once again Masse cursed himself, knowing he should have verified the validity of the document. His carelessness, the result of his trusting comfort level based on a long history of utilizing Zahn's services, had almost, in one moment, undone the years of groundwork Masse had laid.

His mistake. Never trust members of the crime syndicates, they would sell their own mothers for the right price. However in spite of the fact the documents had been forged, Masse now had Argolan exactly where he wanted him. That young man he held meant more to Argolan than his own life. This might actually work out even better than his original game plan. Masse intuited that Julian was weak. He could sense it the way an animal can sense fear in its prey. He would break Julian, then mine him for every piece of information that he could. Argolan would never have broken.

Yes, Masse had lost his soul years ago, and now, in the face of this lie, as Parsons looked into Masse's eyes, he could sense the danger he was in. He decided to drop the matter, for now.

"It was an ambush, Parsons. Argolan had a regiment of security guards outside of the room we went to… 'we' meaning Argolan, Julian Paul, Captain Donahue and me. When we got there, Argolan grabbed my sidearm and executed Donahue. I was able to wrestle the gun from him and hit him over the head with it, but by that time, security guards were coming into the room. I grabbed Paul and used him as leverage to get away."

Parsons said nothing as they walked to the bridge, and although there was no physical evidence to contradict Masse's story, the eyes told him everything. Parsons knew that this was a dangerous man and that he was better off holding his peace.

When Masse and Parsons arrived at the command bridge, it was buzzing with activity.

"Report, Ensign," Masse ordered.

"We have four heavily armed Trade Empire ships on radar. They will be within firing range in three minutes. There is a fifth ship ascending one of the launch corridors from Sharanda. ETA ninety seconds."

While is true that the Empire's ships were designed for salvage, with all of the interplanetary wars and all of the pirate activity in the Galaxy, one cannot traverse space unarmed. Argolan had really taken this idea to heart. The Trade Empire's ships were extremely well-armed.

"You fool, Argolan, *you* should have taken *me* while *I* was in the launch corridor," Masse muttered with a chuckle.

Masse took over. "Ensign, bring our port batteries in line with the corridor. When that window opens I want a clear shot down to the surface."

"Yes, sir."

As the command ship moved into position, the Trade Empire ship's approach seemed to last an eternity. Finally the window which had shielded it opened.

Masse pushed a button on the computer panel which stood in front of the captain's chair which he now occupied. "All batteries fire at the ship."

The corridor lit up with pulses from the laser turrets on the command ship. Sections of the approaching ship exploded, yet it kept coming.

"Direct your fire at the starboard thrusters on the lower decks."

With the destruction of the starboard thrusters, the ship could no longer lift through Sharanda's gravitational field and began to fall back down the launch corridor gently at first, then gathering speed. Within five seconds, the ship had picked up considerable speed and began to ricochet off the sides of the corridor. Fire filled the corridor as the ship plummeted. Sections of the ship separated, becoming fireballs raining down toward Mount Efil. When the ship hit the doors of the hangar from which it was launched, it imploded. The launch corridor shielding disappeared, and something unexpected happened.

A series of explosions occurred throughout Mount Efil which could be seen from the command ship's orbit. Masse was at the same time thrilled and concerned. He was thrilled that he had just crippled Argolan's prized Mount Efil, but he was also concerned that Argolan may have been killed in the process.

"No, Argolan," Masse thought to himself, "You can't die this easily."

"Ensign, set a course for the No'on system, and engage light drive."

Chapter 16

Shockwave

Argolan came to. One of the members of his security force was hunched over him stitching his head.

"Oh," moaned Argolan.

"Sir, he's up," the medic called to his squad manager. "Don't move. You have a pretty nasty cut."

As the squad manager approached Argolan, Argolan perked up a little. "Chris, please report."

"Masse's got Julian. We tried to pursue, but he blew the northern hallway. As it is, we're going to have to take the passages through the Southern Quarter to get back to command. I cannot reach our security squad in the hangar bay and I'm concer……….."

Suddenly they heard an incredibly loud screeching sound like nails scraping on a chalk board and the ground began to shake. "It's a shockwave!" Chris Connors the security squad's manager yelled as he leapt onto Argolan, shielding him from potential danger.

There was a deafening bang. The direction of the airflow in the room shifted one-hundred-eighty degrees. The hangar doors did not make an airtight seal. They didn't need to as the launch corridor shields did. However, these corridors extended more than five hundred miles upward through the atmosphere and, as a result, were so voluminous they had air currents which ran within them.

The air shifted.

Normally air currents within Mt Efil ran primarily toward the facility's various hangers. Usually the closest hanger to a given area determined the direction of the current. Now, however, at least in the auxiliary room, air was flowing away from the only nearby hangar.

A deafening rumbling sound ensued. Forthwith, the northern door exploded inward, shattering into sand grain sized particles. Argolan and his protector were thrown fifteen feet to the southern end of the room and were only stopped there by the wall. All the other members of the security squad were also hurled across the room. The force of concussion disoriented Argolan, but he was alive. The northern door must have absorbed most of the shock, because based on its condition, they all should have been torn apart by the shockwave.

Suddenly Argolan heard another series of explosions. The first was very loud and sounded close, but gradually the explosions got softer and softer and sounded farther and farther away. The lights went out.

"Oh brother," Argolan thought. "What's next?"

"Chris?"

Nothing.

"Chris?"

Nothing

"Chris!!!"

Nothing.

"Anyone?"

Nothing.

Argolan felt around until he located one of his men. He searched him using only his tactile sense until he found the man's flashlight. Argolan stood up and turned it on. He moved the beam of light frantically around the room looking for any sign of life. When he could see none, Argolan slowed down his search pattern. It was gruesome. Most of the men were badly lacerated from the particles of the door. Some of their clothing and most of their exposed flesh had been sandblasted off. A couple of the men had been flung into the southern wall, but they hadn't been as lucky as Argolan. Where these two men had hit the wall, some sections of the rock had separated leaving jagged, spear-like protrusions. Their limp bodies still hung there.

Argolan began searching, almost in a panic, for Chris Connors. He was there. So much of the skin had been sandblasted from his back that some of his ribcage was exposed. Argolan knew that he only stood there because of Chris's sacrifice. Instead of trying to run and save himself, Chris had willingly given his life to save Argolan's. Tears welled in Argolan's eyes.

Only then did Argolan become acutely aware of pain in his legs. He turned the flashlight downward to see that his legs were not in much better shape than were the corpses in the room. Feeling quite faint, he crumpled to the ground. His thoughts became fuzzy, and his eyes rolled back in his head.

Chapter 17

The Prize

Julian sat in a plush chair in the corner of Masse's ostentatious quarters. Priceless tapestries made of the finest cloth covered most of the walls. The bed was on a handmade wrought iron frame with an antique canopy. Beautiful mahogany book shelves were filled with books about military strategy and the administration of battle.

This had been a long, troublesome day so Julian attempted to use his time sitting to recompose himself. His rest came to an abrupt end when he felt the shockwaves from a series of explosions. He jumped up and looked out the porthole to find the source but couldn't see anything except the expanse of space so he sat back down.

Julian's stomach had the nervous feeling one experiences when he knows he is to meet his doom. He was not scared of death. Julian was good with the Lord. He had spent his life attempting to live righteously. He had recently told his friends and family (except for Faith) that he loved them, so there were no unresolved relationships. However, he was scared of the journey to death on which he was about to embark. He had looked into the eyes of this man Masse, and all that he saw was animus. There was blind hatred and anger such as Julian had never before seen, now he was caught directly between the Serpent and its prey.

Julian could not imagine himself standing up to an interrogation. He would betray his father, the man he loved more than anyone else in the Galaxy, his hero, not long into the interrogation. Julian knew this.

Coward.

What would Argolan do? Every time he was faced with difficulty he prayed. He thanked the Lord for what he had and asked for His help.

Julian stood and then knelt on the floor with his arms folded in prayer. "Lord," he began, "I thank You for this day. I thank You for the family into which You placed me when my parents died. Please assure them of how much I love them and will miss them. Comfort them in my absence until we are reunited in Your kingdom. And lastly, please give me the courage to face what is to come with dignity. I love You and Your Son, and I thank You for all the blessings You have given me in my life. Please forgive me for my sins. I say these things in the name of Jesus Christ. Amen."

A peace unlike anything Julian had ever experienced came over him as he finished the prayer. For the first time in his life, the coward took a back seat as a courageous hero emerged. Julian slowly stood, stretched, and then returned to the seat in which he had been resting before his prayer.

As the doors of Masse's quarters opened, Julian felt a shiver run down his spine. Face-to-face with the Serpent again. Just the proximity of Masse was enough to make every hair on Julian's body stand on end. How was Argolan always so composed when staring this monstrosity in the face? The peace, the courage that had comforted Julian just moments before, never left. It did, however, allow a strong sense of foreboding to remain with the Serpent's presence. He was now able to sense evil for what it was, and finally, he had the courage to confront it.

Masse smirked at Julian. "Your father may be dead. Our escape proved somewhat sloppier than I would have hoped."

"You'll never get away with this," Julian calmly said. "The military will never let you."

"You really are quite naive," Masse interrupted. "The military is controlled, albeit unofficially, by the Guild. The Guild is plotting to take control of the Trade Empire. This is the only corner of the Galaxy in which the Guild's control is not absolute. The Guild has allowed it to remain so. Sharanda is to be the Guild's outer seat of power. Mankind has spread too far out of the Terran System to control the New Territories from Old Earth.

"And then of course, there is the Norson Expanse. Due to the Expanse it has been far too costly to extend the full power of the Republic out here. And Sigma Commerce Bureau aside, there needs to be complete infrastructure in place out here. Argolan has done that work neatly for the Republic. But he is not their man. He knows that. The Guild knows that. I have.......contacts in the Guild who have authorized my action here. You see, if I take down Argolan, arrest or discredit him, I solve a huge problem for the Guild. The Empire will not be able to hold itself together without Argolan and will crave new leadership. That is where the Guild will step in, simply utilizing the infrastructure which he created."

In truth, the Guild held Masse in a complex web of strings as though he were a marionette. It knew that he didn't care at all about the cause. The Guild observed him carefully. If he wandered one degree off of the desired course, the Guild would sever his strings and let him fall. The trick was to enable Masse to *feel* empowered and in charge while he was actually maneuvered to achieve the Guild's ends. This had been done prodigiously.

"The Empire will never submit to Guild control, especially if you kill Argolan in the process," asserted Julian.

"My destroying Argolan is not part of the Guild's process! My goals and those of the Guild just have a beautiful synergy up until that point, enabling me to go about my plan with the Guild believing I am fulfilling its plan. That is why I have been granted such latitude. That is why this has been the course of my plans for almost thirty years now. Once I expose the fullness of my plan to the Guild, by killing Argolan, the Guild will have me executed for treason."

"You're insane."

"Perhaps, but I am about to have all of my dreams come to fruition. Can you say the same of yourself?" Masse paused. "Guards!"

Two SEALs entered.

"Rebind his hands and take him to interrogation room four."

One of the SEALs grabbed Julian's arms and pulled them behind his back while the other placed the force binders on them. One SEAL walked ahead while the second SEAL escorted Julian with his left hand on Julian's upper arm. As Julian was led down the hallway to the interrogation room, everything once again seemed to be moving in slow motion. He knew that this would be the last time that he would see anything other than the inside of that room.

Eventually the SEAL who walked ahead of Julian and his escort opened a door to the right. The escort urged him into the room and told him to sit. It was very warm. There was little light in the room. There was a table, a chair that looked like a leftover from a grade-school classroom, a computer cart with a spotlight on it, and a frame that looked like something from the Focus' science lab. The SEALs turned off the lights, rendering the interrogation room completely dark, and exited.

Perspiration streamed down Julian's temples, ran down his cheeks and dripped off him. Based on the sound, the droplets hit the table.

Julian waited for the Serpent to come. And he waited. And waited. After what seemed like an eternity, the door opened and a figure walked in. Julian couldn't distinguish who it was as the light from outside of the room blinded him. A second figure entered, and the doors shut.

Julian's heart jumped as an extremely bright light suddenly shone directly into his eyes. The light instantly gave him a headache. It also further heated up the already hot room.

A silhouette came forth from behind the light. It grabbed his head with its right hand and tilted it back. Once Julian's head was back, the silhouette pulled a container from its left jacket pocket and administered drops of some liquid from the container. Julian attempted to keep his eyes closed but the silhouette grabbed his eyelids one at a time with its hands and forced them open. Julian blinked as the drops made their way into his eyes. The figure returned to behind the light where it could not be seen.

As Julian waited, there wasn't a sound. He couldn't even hear the others breathing. Suddenly, however, he became acutely aware of his own breathing. It became labored. He struggled for air. His pupils dilated, making the light absolutely blinding, and he began to feel nauseated.

Feeling even hotter than before, Julian thought he was going to lose consciousness. His thinking was becoming unfocused. Every breath became a greater struggle, he lost his equilibrium. As the room spun faster and faster, Julian suddenly realized that he was no longer sitting in the chair but, lying on his back on the floor. He couldn't remember falling from the chair. He had a searing pain in the back of his head. He was sweating profusely, causing his clothing to become wet and stick to him. While the real torture hadn't even begun, this was probably the most disturbing feeling Julian had ever experienced- barring, of course, his inability to act in the face of his parents' demise.

He hadn't sensed the silhouette come toward him but it was pulling him up by his upper arms. It placed him back in the chair.

The Serpent spoke. "What is your name?"

Julian found himself responding without even trying to. "Julian Paul."

"Who is your father?"

Again Julian responded without any conscious thought on his part. "Argolan."

"Where is the Trade Empire's seat of power?"

"Mount Efil, Sharanda."

"What is the name of the ship you command?"

"The Liahona."

"Tell me about the last operation you ran. You were in the Ranis System?"

Now the Serpent was beginning to probe. He was starting to ask questions, which in his normal frame of mind, Julian wouldn't even consider answering. Without hesitation he replied, "Yes."

"What did you find there?"

"Normal war-theater salvage items." Julian resisted. He gave a very simplified version of the truth.

"Did you have all of the required permits and permissions?"

"Yes."

"Were all licenses obtained legally and due fees given to the Guild?"

"Yes."

The Serpent growled.

"Were any human remains desecrated or treated in a disrespectful manner?"

A slight hesitation. "No."

The Serpent paused to consider the hesitation. "Was he lying or just resisting," the Serpent wondered. "Were all Galactic laws governing salvage followed to the letter?"

Julian fought, attempting not to answer but he couldn't stop himself. "Yes."

The Serpent paused. "Increase the room's temperature by five degrees," he instructed the silhouette.

The Serpent waited as the increased temperature worked on Julian. Feeling extremely disoriented and more nauseous Julian began to lose consciousness once again. Instantaneously, the silhouette came forward, smelling salts in hand, placing it under Julian's nose. This woke him up.

Julian now felt slightly reinvigorated. "Lord," he prayed, "Please let Your Spirit be with me that I will be able to resist."

"You hesitated, Mr. Paul. Which laws did your crew break?"

Julian's crew hadn't broken any laws. That is not how Argolan ran his business. Ultimate integrity. Nonetheless, with renewed vigor, Julian refused to answer.

"You will not get anything from me."

The Serpent sighed. "Move him to the cage," he ordered the silhouette.

The silhouette came forth. Its right hand grabbed Julian's right upper arm and yanked him up to a standing position. It then went around behind Julian and unbound his hands.

"Put your hands out in front of you," commanded the silhouette. Julian complied, while at the same time praying for strength and poise.

The silhouette reactivated the force binders, restraining Julian's hands in front of him this time, and led him into the dark frame while the Serpent walked over to the computer cart and turned on a small spotlight in order to see the control panel. The Serpent pushed a few buttons, and a force hook appeared. The hook, reminiscent of a meat hook, dropped down from the top border of the cage until it hovered about seven-and-a-half feet above the floor. The silhouette led Julian to it, pulled his hands up over his head, and lifted him by the binders until he was suspended from the hook. Julian's feet touched the floor, but barely. He knew that this wasn't going to be pleasant.

The silhouette administered more eye drops to Julian while the Serpent worked at the computer station. When he finally glimpsed the silhouette, Julian would have laughed if he hadn't been in such great pain. He was short, skinny and quite geek-like.

At last the silhouette withdrew as the Serpent finished writing his macro program on the work terminal. Now cackling, the Serpent stepped forward toward Julian. Julian could no longer focus his eyes. He was beginning to feel susceptible again, hot, dizzy and nauseous.

"I have waited years for this. You, my friend, are Argolan's Achilles' heel. You will answer my questions. But first, it's time for me to enjoy myself. Think of this as a vacation. Not yours, of course, but mine. You are watching some man, me, from afar while he is enjoying that vacation. He hasn't a trouble in the Galaxy, just the ecstasy that he is experiencing on that long-awaited vacation.'

Then to the computer station the Serpent said, "Run program Masse Alpha One."

A hologram of Julian, much like the hologram of the case on the Focus, appeared on the other end of the cage. The Serpent walked over to the computer station and pulled a pair of gloves out of one of the cabinet's drawers.

"Engage energy grapplers."

With the last command, two force fields came to life in the shape of a pair of hands. To Julian, it was like a dream to watch these hands following Masse's every move. As Masse approached the hologram of Julian, the energy grapplers moved toward Julian.

Julian kept glancing at the hologram of himself. It was almost like watching himself in a video monitor while being filmed with a camera. The hologram reproduced every move he made with perfect likeness.

"Now, Mr. Paul, what laws did your crew break on your salvage mission in the Ranis system?"

Julian prayed for strength. He knew that he was about to be put through pain unlike any he had ever known, but he had no idea how bad it would become.

He wanted to resist but couldn't. He was weak and sweating profusely. He couldn't focus his mind. Just hearing the Serpent's voice was too much. He wanted it to stop. The room was spinning. He started to fight for breath once again.

Julian prayed for the power to resist answering, but he could not. "None. We did everything by the letter of the law."

"You're lying!" And with that the Serpent swung a fist at the hologram.

As the energy grappler struck Julian across the left cheek, he could hear a few of his teeth shatter. Blood dripped from his mouth.

Julian had been hit before, but this was different. When the energy grappler struck him, it was not flesh-like at all. The concussive quality of the strike resembled being hit with a rock. It also sent a shock through his body, leaving his side tingling.

"Let's try this again. What laws did your crew break?"

"None."

The next shot connected with Julian just below his solar plexus. He started to lose consciousness. Again the geek came forward and revitalized Julian.

"We are going to try something a little different, Mr. Paul. I don't know how familiar you are with human physiology, but there are a group of nerves that come out of the thoracic region of the spinal column and follow the ribs around to the front of the body. From there they go into the sternum. When these nerves become aggravated in the back, they send a shooting a pain around to the front that could best be described as a burning sensation. Not just a slight burning sensation, but an agonizing, horrendous, debilitating, oppressive pain which culminates in the sternum feeling as though a weight were on the chest. An unbearable weight. This sensation is so painful that the average human being can only tolerate it for a few seconds before being rendered unconscious. That, my friend, is what you are about to experience."

"Lord," Julian prayed, "please let me die with dignity."

"Disengage energy grappler tactile function," the Serpent commanded the computer. Then he did something Julian had never contemplated. The Serpent plunged his gloved hands into the back of the hologram. As the Serpent went through this routine, the finger tips of the energy grapplers dove into Julian's back. He couldn't feel them. It was almost like passing one's hand through a beam of light. The hand can go into the beam, but there was no discernable tactile contact between the two. These hands were now in Julian's back as though they were mere beams of light. Julian tried to move but didn't have the strength. He couldn't even lift his head up for more than a moment.

Once the Serpent's hands were positioned he said, "Reengage energy grappler tactile function."

The Serpent had underestimated the pain. It was exactly like he had described it, only infinitely worse. Julian let out a sustained scream. The pain in his sternum was like nothing he had ever imagined. He continued screaming until the Serpent removed his hands.

He walked over to Julian smiling. "This is just a taste of what you're in for. I figure to keep you alive for years, if possible, just so I can enjoy this again and again."

Masse removed the gloves he wore, dropped them to the floor and walked toward the exit. When he was almost to door, he stopped and without turning around, said as though it were simply an afterthought, "End program Masse Alpha One." He then left the room. The hook disappeared and Julian fell to the floor.

End Part 1

Chapter 18

War Ensemble

Argolan wasn't certain if it was the talking that woke him or not. His eyes popped open, but he didn't move. He knew where he was, yet didn't understand how he had gotten there. Turning his head to the right, Argolan saw Gabriel, sitting next to his bed in the prayer posture with arms folded and head down.

When he noticed Argolan staring at him, Gabriel's face lit up with an enormous smile. He stood and asked, "How do you feel?"

Argolan reciprocated with a little smile of his own, but he couldn't speak. He just shook his head slightly.

Argolan drifted in and out of sleep. Gabriel was there each time Argolan awoke. When Argolan finally sat up, a buzz arose in the room. He was in the infirmary, but for how long had he been there?

Argolan turned to Gabriel and asked, "How long?" Even this small sentence was a struggle.

"A little more than three weeks."

"J-J-Julian?"

Gabriel shook his head and let it drop.

Argolan's heart dropped into his stomach. "Dead?"

"We don't know. Masse took him, but there has been no attempt to contact us…as far as we know."

"Know?" Argolan forced out.

"Mount Efil is still only running at fifty percent. The shockwave that was created when the Spirit crashed down the launch corridor devastated the southern hangar. That launch corridor is inoperative, and the following explosions knocked out key systems throughout Mount Efil."

"Explosions."

"Yeah. The secondary explosions were our weapons caches exploding due to the shockwave."

"Huh," was all Argolan could manage.

Argolan had seen for years that the next move on the part of the Guild was going to be to execute a military "conversion" of the Trade Federation. The Guild's military had strategic control of ninety percent of the Galaxy, with the only structure in the remaining ten percent being the Trade Empire, aside from the small Republic presence of the Sigma Commerce Bureau. Of course, even between the two, there were still holes. Most of these holes were where the wars were being fought, in systems such as the Ranis system. While Ranis was in imperially controlled space, the Empire had no direct presence there. The Guild's most significant power grab would be to take the Empire. That was the sole reason the Guild's government minions had not interfered as excessively with the Trade Empire's business as with other businesses. The Guild would let the Empire expand and put an infrastructure in place. Once that infrastructure was built out enough, the Guild would seize control of it. This is a typical tactic of military dictators. Find proxies to do your dirty work.

Several years ago, while on a prayerful fast, all of the nebulous pieces of Galactic politics that Argolan hadn't been able to fit together in his mind for the past twenty years suddenly made sense. This was doubtlessly an inspired revelation. From that day forth, the Trade Empire began to build weapons stocks and to arm its vessels, both highly illegal tactics. Argolan had always followed the law strictly, but he had more than one hundred thousand people in his stewardship, and he saw a war coming. The Guild's purpose in that war would be to destroy them (the people) and to seize control of the machine (the Empire's Galactic infrastructure) that they had built. This was not acceptable.

Masse was not part of this war. He had his own war with Argolan. His purposes were not one with that of the Guild. In fact, if Argolan's guess was right, Masse had just become a great liability to the Guild.

Now Masse was exposed, Julian was gone, the Trade Federation's armaments were destroyed, and the nerve center of the Federation was severely crippled. This had been a difficult time.

Argolan fell back to sleep.

A few days later Argolan awoke early in the morning feeling like a new man. He had a purpose. That purpose was to save his son, if, he was still alive, at any cost.

That afternoon he was up and around. He took a deep breath before entering the main conference room which was located just outside the Command Center. Argolan entered, and silence fell over the chatty crowd. As Argolan made his way to his chair at the head of the table the more than two hundred sitting leaders of the Trade Empire stood and applauded him. Argolan felt a little uneasy at this outpouring of love. Did he really deserve it? After all, he had just let these people down severely when Masse came.

The ovation continued for a few minutes until Argolan was at last able to get everybody to stop applauding and return to their seats.

"We have full schedule, my friends, and no time for this. But I am touched."

As Argolan sat at the head of the enormous conference table, much of his leadership was concerned that he was already pushing himself too hard, that he wasn't yet ready to return to work. However, they also knew that Argolan was a determined individual, that if he felt he was ready, none would be able to dissuade him.

"Marco, in Ms. Chase's absence, would you please begin by reporting on the state of the Empire?"

Marco Toms, the assistant director of operations for the Empire stood at his seat. He pushed a button on the computer panel on his place at the table and the lights dimmed. A hologram appeared above the center of the oval table. The hologram was a topographical map of the interior of Mount Efil.

"It has been almost a month since the attack. As you can see, much of Mount Efil's infrastructure is still inoperable. Our long-range radar is still inoperative. Communications was restored only recently, and we have dozens of ships, which we are unable to contact, out on missions. We lost key personnel. The launch corridors on the southern ends of Mount Efil are not working, and of course the southern hangar and all ships which were docked there are destroyed. It's bad. It will take us years to recover fully."

Argolan sighed. These all were superficial problems. If the Guild's onslaught was going to begin, they would all be dead shortly, with no way of defending themselves.

"What about our armaments?" Argolan asked.

Marco sat down and deferred to Naziz Kumar, the Trade Empire's security director. In an ideal world, Argolan would not have had his security director running the effort to build the Empire's ability to wage war. Internal security and external war are two completely different disciplines. But the Trade Empire was not a military organization, and this was not a perfect world. Argolan could foresee that over the coming months and years many people would have to learn to take on new roles. The challenge with this shift in responsibilities was that if Naziz wasn't great in his new roll, every man, woman, and child affiliated with the Trade Empire would die. Naziz knew this and he had worked diligently over the past several years to school himself in the art of war. He had gained enormous respect from within the Empire as a result.

Kumar stood. "The shockwave that the impact of the Spirit created triggered some of the less stable elements of our weapons caches to detonate. Like a domino effect, this in turn caused the next cache to explode which caused the next cache to explode. In retrospect, the caches were placed too close together. These secondary explosions killed dozens and wounded hundreds of people. We have no military strength left other than our ships being heavily armed, a few tactical nuclear weapons and a fair supply of laser pistols. Those won't carry us very far against an invasion by the Navy. I agree with Marco's assessment. It will take years to rebuild."

Next Argolan addressed Lawrence Young, the ATS Focus's commander.

"Lawrence, has there been any progress made with the study of the alien technology that the Focus acquired?"

Young stood up to address the room. "No. We know that it is immeasurably advanced over our own technology. In fact, it is so advanced that we have made no headway with it at all."

Various conversations of different topics relevant to the state of the Empire went on for almost two more hours, at which time Argolan decided it was prudent to commence with the spectacular finale he had planned.

"Before opening the floor to the general audience I have a plan I want to set into motion now," he proclaimed.

Argolan observed everyone's reaction. He had gotten their attention, and he proceeded.

"We are going to find Julian. I thi-"

The room roared with applause. Not just short, polite applause, but sustained uproarious applause. This was a group displaying its love for Julian.

When the excitement finally died down, Argolan continued, "I don't know if he is alive o.. or..dead.." Argolan choked up and had to wait a moment to continue, "But either way, we are going to find him and bring him back. This is not a condition of your employment with the Trade Empire, none of you are required to help me in this endeavor. I am asking you, as friends, for volunteers to help me in this most perilous mission."

Gabriel was the first to stand up, followed by Young. Of course Gabriel standing first was no surprise, as he and Julian were best friends, but Young? Young did not like Julian. He felt that Julian had usurped a lot of the spotlight he should have received for helping to build the Trade Empire into what it had become. The truth was that while Young might not have liked Julian, he loved Argolan and he could see the anguish this was causing him.

One by one people continued to stand until finally everyone in the room was standing. Argolan was touched.

"Where do we begin?" someone yelled.

Argolan responded. "Excellent question. Gabriel."

"Me?" was Gabriel's confused response.

"Yes. You have family involved in the Oralti Crime Syndicate, don't you?"

"Yes, they run it."

"The documents that Masse brought here with him contained something in them which indicated that we need to begin our search in the Sigma System. Your family may be able to get us information that no one else will be able to. Would you please make contact?"

Gabriel became agitated; this idea concerned him. Those people couldn't be trusted. Finally he spoke. "I wouldn't know how to reach them."

Argolan's intuition told him that this might not be entirely true but he knew how much Gabriel cared for Julian. It was safe to assume therefore that if Gabriel felt he could do what Argolan was asking of him, he would.

"All right Gabriel, we will put the Empire's resources on it."

Chapter 19

A New Threat

"Does anyone have anything else to add?" asked Argolan. As if by providence, at that moment, Trent Seigers, Managing Director of the Cryptography and Intelligence Center, entered the room waving a paper report. "I have some information I would like to share with this body."

"Proceed," Argolan replied.

"In your absence the Cryptography and Intelligence Center deciphered the language on the device that the Focus found on the derelict and translated its contents."

If Seiger's entrance hadn't, this grabbed the attention of the whole room.

"The object was a journal belonging to the ship's first officer. It contained personal entries, historical documents, literature, poetry, and among other things, the derelict's cargo manifest. This manifest includes the object in the case. It is a component of a weapon. Apparently it was a weapon of such unbelievably destructive power that when the race that created it was, shall we say 'defeated,' the components of the weapon were dispersed across the Galaxy and hidden so the weapon could never be rebuilt."

"Wait, wait, wait. How could a race with such a weapon be defeated?" Argolan probed.

"The log did not include too much detail on this subject other than to say they were more tricked than defeated. The armies of another other race deceived the creators of this weapon and dismantled it. They shipped its components, which were irreplaceable, to all ends of the Galaxy so that the weapon could never be reconstructed. But that's not the amazing part of the story."

"Of course not," Argolan said. Lately nothing had been as simple as a genocidal race of aliens with a weapon of mass destruction powerful enough to change the Galaxy completely.

"Here is the unbelievable part. The radiation that Sharanda naturally creates is the very kind that powered this weapon. That is why when Abraham lowered the shield that day on the Focus, the component came to life. Routine maintenance was begun in Hangar 2N's shields just after the Focus landed. The radiation permeating the hangar was being blocked by the controlled area's shielding. When Kalman lowered the shield, the energy came into contact with the component, and it was reactivated."

"How do we know this?"

"Apparently this officer whose journal we obtained had a strong background in science. On a side note, this war between these two races had been a multi-generational affair. Certain individuals were schooled in things of this nature. That is probably part of what got him to the position of first officer. Anyway, getting back to my point, there were technical documents in his journal which we took down to our science team. They studied the descriptions and documentation in the log, of the energy that powered the weapon, utilizing the translation guidelines the Center developed. The only energy patterns our scientists have seen before which are remotely similar are the energy patterns created by our little homestead here, and they were an exact match."

Argolan glanced over to see Young shifting uncomfortably in his seat, obviously uneasy about his unawareness of the report which had just been delivered. Argolan gave him a reassuring smile and returned to his conversation with Seigers.

"That is unbelievable. What are the odds?" Argolan asked.

"There's more," Seigers continued, "After the component is powered by this energy source, it converts the energy. In this process, the inputted energy is converted and the device gives off a new kind of energy signature. This is a very low band signature. It travels for a long, long distance without being inhibited."

"Yes, we know that. Some of our ships which were far away were affected by the pulse it sent out."

"That's just it, Argolan. In his journal, the first officer talks about the enemy race hunting down the components of the weapon. They are killers, killing machines of perfection, to be more exact. There is a good chance that they detected the pulse. There is also a good chance that they are on their way here to collect their property."

There was a collective gasp in the room.

Argolan tried not to show any emotion. Many of his leaders would be looking to him as an example of how to lead their people through this time. Inside Argolan was crushed. This was a most perilous time the Trade Empire was entering. The animus of all of its enemies seemed to be converging, just as its defenses were crushed.

"Abraham," Argolan addressed the Empire's top-ranking scientist, "Can you offer any further insight into this race's technological strength?"

Kalman stood up to address Argolan. "Argolan, you've seen their technology. In a month, with the exception of the one weapon part, we haven't been able to even begin to understand how any of it works. If they come for us........."

Kalman's voice drifted off.

Chapter 20

The Ghost

As Gabriel sat in the command chair of the Liahona, he looked out the foreword viewer at Sigma seventeen which encompassed the entire horizon. It gave him goose bumps. However, the emotions that would normally be elicited by this amazing sight were eclipsed by a sense of emptiness.

Julian.

Having never been on board the Liahona when it was in space without him, Gabriel realized just how much he missed Julian. It just wasn't the same. Gabriel had analyzed the facts many times in his mind and realized it likely would never be the same again.

But relations had been changing recently between Julian and Gabriel. Their relationship had become…uneasy, at least in Gabriel's mind. He didn't know if Julian had sensed it or not. It was mostly over a political divide between them. Gabriel saw the writing on the wall. Gabriel understood that if the Empire would just sit down with the Guild and submit to some admittedly constraining guidelines, the two powers could coexist peacefully. Unfortunately Julian and Argolan were somewhat aggressive in their views of Galactic politics. They believed that a war with the Guild was inevitable. They had no desire to be flexible and live peacefully under Guild control. Their war-mongering attitudes would likely be the end of the Empire and cost thousands of people their lives. Still Gabriel dearly loved and missed Julian.

Although it had tried, the Trade Empire's efforts to make contact with an operative of the Oralti Crime Syndicate had been going too slowly. These crime organizations survived by keeping a very low profile. The Empire had called in many favors and even put political pressure on some local Galafon law enforcement organizations, to no avail. It was only when Gabriel finally acquiesced and used his private contacts that they were finally able to get a name and coding for contact with the Syndicate.

When the Trade Empire's armada had entered the Sigma System, Gabriel sent a coded communiqué to his contact requesting a channel of communication with his uncle who ran the syndicate (according to his father many years ago). It had been many hours now, and there was still no response to the request. It was time to wait.

Gabriel knew that as the showdown with Masse approached, so likely did the end of his life. The Trade Federation's armada was a joke at best being comprised of six ships. Six ships against Masse's Fifth Fleet, which was renowned throughout the Galaxy. Gabriel never liked a fight that was fifteen hundred to six against him, but he liked it even less when the fifteen hundred was the Fifth Fleet. These soldiers had been trained like no others. The Fleet's pilots were the best in the Galaxy, and their gunners… In all, the Fifth Fleet was battle-hardened and equipped to the hilt.

The funny thing was that Gabriel didn't care. All he cared about was closure, putting that final touch on the relationship he had built with his life-long friend. In reality though, attaining even that was a long shot.

Suddenly the communications computer chirped, signaling an incoming message, requesting Gabriel's key. He typed his security key into the computer and an image came to life on the viewer which nearly caused him to fall out of the chair in which he sat. Gabriel's father had told him of his brother, but he never mentioned that they were identical twins. For Gabriel, looking at his uncle was like seeing a ghost. He was speechless.

"Little One, it's good to meet you. You are the spitting image of your father."

"So are you!" Gabriel managed to squeak out.

The man chuckled. "Your father never told you we were identical twins. Charming." Accompanying his speech were many exaggerated hand motions.

"It must have slipped his mind." Gabriel was still off balance.

"I have been aware of you since you were born. I kept....tabs on your parents over the years. I was happy for them when they had you. I was happy for their success in the Trade Empire and I am happy that you have grown into such a dignified man. I was saddened to hear of your parents' deaths. I think...." The man's words trailed off. His eyes narrowed and a look of skepticism came over his face.

"Why are you here?" the man asked.

"We would like to request an audience with you."

"Why?"

"My brother has been abducted and our only clue as to where he may be brings us to Sigma Organized Crime syndicates."

"Brother?"

"Not blood," Gabriel clarified. "Lifelong best friend."

"I don't believe you. Who is the man you seek?"

This astonished Gabriel. Gabriel had been coached by Argolan. Argolan knew that Gabriel had led a somewhat sheltered life and tended to trust everybody, in fact, to disclose too much. Argolan instructed him that one could never trust a member of any of the crime syndicates. The only time that one even deals with a syndicate member is when there is absolutely no other choice. And then one must be careful because the criminal will stab one in the back to make a profit the second one lets one's guard down (just as Zahn had to Masse). Finally, Argolan had instructed Gabriel that under NO CIRCUMSTANCES could the crime syndicate find out who it was that the Armada was seeking because the syndicate would understand the value of capturing Julian for itself.

"He is no one of any great consequence, other than being my good friend," Gabriel bluffed. He was extremely nervous being less than truthful, but he understood the stakes. He attempted to project a calm façade.

"Little One, I am going to give you one more chance to come clean. If you fail to do so, I am going to end this communication. The Argalian Trade Empire would not send its flagship with this little fleet without due cause." The man raised his voice to reflect the intonation of a parent scolding his child. "My patience is almost exhausted."

Now Gabriel was perplexed. How had the man identified Argolan's ship? It is unmarked and unassuming. How could he have known? This "fleet" to which the man referred consisted of six ships: The Liahona commanded by Gabriel; the Focus commanded by Young; Argolan's flagship which he commanded and three of the Empire's most heavily armed ships. One would have thought that except to the most insightful of observers, the flagship would have gotten lost in the shuffle.

"All right, but you may not like the answer. This friend of mine was abducted by Admiral James Masse of the Fifth Fleet. We are at a very dangerous point where if we're not careful, this could cause a large-scale incident. I'm sorry that I didn't disclose this to you right away, but I was concerned that you would shy away from the politics of the situation."

"You are asking a lot, Little One." The man sighed.

"I'm begging you. This man has been with me through most of my life." Again Gabriel thought of the rift that had been emerging between them, but he didn't allow any outward signs of doubt to show.

"Because you are my blood, you may bring an unarmed party of five to Sigma Twelve where I am. Here are the coordinates at which I'll meet you. Use the scanner on the facility's door, it will recognize your DNA" said the man. And then he added something Gabriel never expected. "Oh, yes, and have Argolan join you. I have always wanted to meet him."

How did this man know these things?

Chapter 21

Eden

James Masse sat back in the recliner in his quarters in his fortress on Eden in the No'on system. No'on was an uncharted system until Masse's fleet stumbled on it during the Battle of Tim Byur. A bloody battle in a bloody war.

He had aptly named this world Eden as this was his paradise. It was not exactly the type of paradise which a tourist would seek out for vacation. This was, however, a paradise to Masse, as it would be the base from which he would carry out his plans to bring about the end of Argolan.

The past two months had been exquisite fun for Masse. He knew that if even Argolan had survived the attack on Mount Efil, he did not know whether or not Julian was alive. Argolan's Empire had also been crippled. This had been sweet, even if it had not worked out quite the way Masse had planned.

Masse had modeled his fortress after Mount Efil with one major difference: It was under water. Mount Efil was protected by radiation emitted by Sharanda as well as its stone walls. It was unique. However, there were other ways of shielding a compound besides radiation.

It had taken the team of geologists Masse had hired two years of work to complete mapping out the ocean floors of Eden. Once done, he brought in a group of structural engineers. Together they determined the most well-protected site on the ocean floor in which to build an underwater city.

Construction had taken nearly seven years, but watching the process had been a thrill. The structure was made mostly of stainless steel, titanium and aluminum. The sections were bulbous with connecting tubes. The tubes were made of transparent aluminum, giving one walking through a three-hundred-sixty degree view of the ocean outside. The structure itself was reminiscent of a cage in which people kept pet rodents. The most amazing features, however, were the launch corridors, a concept "borrowed" from Argolan.

Of course space-worthy ships were not equipped for submersion, so Masse had needed to install a launch corridor system. This became the most awe-inspiring part of the construction. When the completed launch corridors were activated, they were full of water. High-pressured air was then forced from within the compound, into the launch corridors. The water in the launch corridors was, for lack of a better term, launched from them.

This fortress was approximately fifty-two miles below the surface, so the volume of water being displaced was phenomenal. From the surface, where Masse observed, it looked as though the whole ocean would be depleted as he watched the water shoot out of the launch corridor and up into the sky. Unlike on Sharanda, where the launch corridors extended into space, there was no need for that here. These launch corridors simply extended to about two hundred feet above the sea's level.

"Music level up to five," Masse said, as he drew a deep, relaxed breath.

Chapter 22

A Well-Lit Meeting

While Argolan's personal shuttle was putting down on Sigma Twelve, the party was unusually quiet. They all understood what a precarious position into which they were about to willingly walk.

Sigma Twelve was a bastion of trade, as was the whole Sigma System. Being under Trade Empire jurisdiction, the Guild's laws had had a relatively small impact on the economy, and this particular section of Sigma Twelve bustled with the evidence. There were markets, bazaars, and traders everywhere lining the streets in their kiosks, even though it was late at night. The buzz of activity never stopped. There were also warehouses everywhere; places in which Sigma Twelve's masters of commerce stored their goods. It was to one of these warehouses that the coordinates Gabriel had received from Williams took them.

The group arrived at its destination, and Gabriel placed his hand over the DNA scanner on the door. It opened. When his uncle had told him that his DNA would be recognized by the scanner, Gabriel had had his doubts. How could he have gotten a DNA sample from Gabriel? How did he do these things?

Upon entering the warehouse, Gabriel and his squadron were careful to make certain that the door was securely closed behind them; they didn't want any unwelcome observers to follow. It was quite dark inside the warehouse. A little light from the activity outside came through two dirty windows near the high ceiling, but there were no lights on inside. The men had just enough light to see where they were going.

When they approached the center of the large room, reaching the supplied coordinates, Gabriel could make out a handful of silhouettes approximately twenty feet in front of them. The lights came on, and now Gabriel stood with Argolan, Young, Dean Bennette (the Liahona's director of security) and Drew Davies (the flagship's director of security) before his uncle, Kasis Williams. The two crews faced each other briefly in silence.

Suddenly Kasis gave Gabriel an inviting smile and took a step towards him, engulfing him in a long, warm embrace. After a few moments Kasis released him and took a couple of steps back. "I have waited for many years to meet you. Tell me about yourself," Kasis demanded, accompanying his words with the most flamboyant hand gestures that Gabriel had ever seen.

This seemed like an odd ice breaker to Gabriel, but this was Kasis's way. He was quirky, having grown up in a family which ran the largest crime syndicate in the Galaxy. His entire life people had catered to his every whim. He had never been told no. He had been raised with servants to meet his every need and always had yes-men to support even his most eccentric ideas as though they were the words of a prophet.

But Gabriel knew all about him and his type of person. His father had told him all about the "princess mentality" which permeated the hierarchy of the syndicates. All others were simply resources. As soon as one became an inconvenience, it was over. In truth, Gabriel resented Kasis and those of his ilk.

Gabriel also did not know how to respond to Kasis's question, as he was not used to being in the spotlight. "There isn't much to tell. I've lived a pretty normal life. As you know, Mom and Dad died when I was quite young, but not too young to take care of myself. I've worked for the Empire all of my adult life. I'm not yet married. However, in spite of the turmoil I have experienced in my life, the one constant throughout has been the companionship of my best friend."

"Hmm," Kasis gave a knowing nod, "Julian Paul."

How did he know these things?

Argolan stepped forward. "Please help us find my son if he's alive, or his body if not."

Kasis smiled at Argolan. "I am a huge admirer of yours and the Empire you have built." Kasis paused for effect, ever the showman. "I am going to help you, but for a price. Understand that I don't give a whit about you or your son. Although I would like to help my nephew, even that would not be enough to compel me to enter into this endeavor with you. I am inserting my organization into a very dangerous situation, a situation which could come back to bite me in the end."

"What price?" asked Argolan.

"Masse has aligned himself with my organization's primary competitor. If the Guild were to align itself with this organization, it would be over for my confederation. We have been keeping our eye on this troubling chain of events for some time now. Masse has cultivated a relationship with a second-tier operative in the Schuelli Family. This man, Zahn, while not a boss, is a top lieutenant in their organization. He sold Masse some forged documents which were supposedly to incriminate your organization. He will know where Masse is. I want him. I want to extract information from him about the exact nature of the relationship between the Schuelli Family's organization and the Guild. We can't get near him. You're going to have to do it. When you do, you are going to bring him to me, and we'll extract the information we need from him."

"I can't do that," said Argolan. "I can not deliver this man to his death."

"Oh, I'm not going to kill him. He has information I need, information which is time-sensitive. *I* will be interrogating him however. I hope you have a strong stomach."

"What if he dies during your interrogation?"

"I will do everything within my power to see that doesn't happen. You have my word."

"Your word?"

"My word. And remember, he can almost certainly lead us to Masse, which will help you to get your son….." Kasis stopped speaking and began flamboyantly waving his hands in the air, "who is still alive, by the way………back."

How did he know these things? Gabriel wondered.

Argolan's knees weakened. Just the thought of seeing Julian alive once more…. But how could he trust Kasis? He couldn't, but he had no choice.

Kasis smiled. He could see on Argolan's face the love he had for his son.

Kasis continued, "We have a starting point from which you will be able to make contact with Zahn. However, I am giving you only the starting point, the rest will be up to you. I cannot help. If I do, it will compromise our stealth."

"Why do you even need me to do this? It sounds as though you already have everything you need."

"Stealth. My organization is on the Schuelli organization's radar. Yours is not. My organization is being watched. We have been planning this rendezvous with you for weeks. I am reasonably certain that we have maintained secrecy. I have woven such an elaborate web leading up to tonight's events that we believe this meeting has gone unnoticed… hopefully…."

"Hopefully" worried Argolan. If Kasis was wrong, Argolan would be killed the instant he came into contact with the Schuelli Family's operatives.

However, Kasis wasn't wrong. The Oralti Crime Syndicate had confined all chatter and organizational operations (except for a select few agents) to another operation, a massive direct assault on the Schuelli Family's main headquarters. The attack was of no greater value than a sleight of hand to enable their meeting to occur in secrecy. It had only had the effect of directing the Schuellis' focus elsewhere.

"We have created an alias for you and have a meeting set with a man who can put you into contact with Zahn." With an exaggerated motion, Kasis reached his right hand into the left breast pocket of his overcoat and pulled out an envelope. "Here is all of the documentation you will need, to get started. Once you have Zahn, you will make contact with me through the same channels which you did originally. We will have no further communication until then."

"Little One, it was good to meet you." Kasis smiled at Gabriel. Gabriel scowled in return. Kasis made another flamboyant hand gesture, and he and his men turned and exited the building though a rear door.

Gabriel turned to Argolan. "You're not going to do this, are you?"

Argolan thought for a moment. "Do we have an option?"

"I don't know, but this man is an animal. We don't want to have anything to do with him. We cannot deliver Zahn to that man."

Argolan did not know what to say. He had sensed an uneasiness growing inside Gabriel over the past months. Argolan knew what Julian meant to him, but Gabriel appeared to have developed a duality of mind.

"I have no intention of turning Zahn over to Kasis. Let's get back to our ships."

Chapter 23

A Look into the Eye of the Beast

As Captain Split Jackson (there is a long story behind his name) looked at the horizon from the deck of the Argalian Hover-Skiff Horizon, he marveled at the colors. He had been to perhaps seventy planets in his life, and Sharanda had by far the most beautiful sunsets. The hover-skiff was used as a sentry patrol for Mount Efil. Of course, since no other ships could fly here, the Horizon never saw any action, but it was used as a due diligence measure to protect the homestead. Since the traditional anti-gravity thrusters which would be used on ships of this sort didn't work on Sharanda, the skiff was a combustion engine-driven vehicle.

Argolan, ever employing his sense of humor, had taken this throwback of technology to the extreme. Not only had he put an antique-style propulsion system on the Horizon, but he went full tilt Old World. The open deck was built with a wood finish resembling the deck of an early Old Earth naval ship, probably in an eighteenth century English style. The piece-de-resistance was a harpoon gun mounted at the very front of the bow. Of course for practical reasons there were also six high caliber conventional machine guns mounted onto the rails of the deck.

The various launch corridors of Mount Efil could be made to have their shields diverted, extending them around the skiff. This enabled the skiff to employ anti-gravity thrusters to work. However, this greatly limited the range of these skiffs. As a result, Argolan had the Imperial Skiffs fitted with silent combustion-driven propulsion engines. Well, silent was not wholly true. They were much quieter than the jet engines which had powered Man's earlier trips into the skies. They did, however, produce a low hum. When a person was first assigned to a skiff's crew, the hum tended to drive him crazy. However, after a while of living with the hum day in and day out, one got used to it, even missed it when it's not present. Captain Jackson had a first-hand testimony of this.

The skiff's crew of six all sat upon the deck of the Horizon taking in the sunset. A Sharanda sunset has explosive colors of red, blue, purple, orange and yellow as a result of its radiation field. They relaxed and enjoyed it.

Jackson looked over at his team lead Oliver Towne. "Are you taking your kids to the ball game this weekend?"

That brought a smile to Oliver's face. "Every weekend. Why don't you and Tina joins us? I'll bring Nancy, and afterward we can go back to our place and have a cookout."

Oliver had two young sons at home. It made Split think back to when his and Tina's daughter was younger and still living at home.

"Nah," Split replied. "You enjoy your time with your family. There is a new Ranasian restaurant open in Empire City that I think we're going to check out."

"Suit yourself." Oliver turned and looked over at their four crewmates. "Any of you guys brave enough to admit that you have no life outside of work and join us with this late notice?" The six men chuckled.

"You know," Split began, "They are supposed to be building a.... new... stadium...... for sp.........." He drifted off.

Off in the distance Split saw something in the sky. He couldn't make out what it was.

"Do any of you see that?" He asked.

"No, what? Where?"

Split extended his right arm, pointing his index finger at the blur off in the distance. The crew confirmed seeing it. They stood in awe, leaning against the port rail of the bow, watching as the blur grew.

Finally Split ordered everyone to the guns. He pulled a communicator from his pocket and clipped it onto his left sleeve.

"Command Center! I need shields now."

"Done, Split," came the response from Deirdre Lane in the Ops Center.

A faint glow now extended from the shields surrounding Mount Efil to encompass the Horizon.

"Deirdre, please put me on speaker to the whole Command Center."

"You're on."

"We can see what appears to be a dark spot in the sky. It's too far out to tell what it is."

No sooner did Split finish his sentence than he knew what it was. In approximately a second, the ship was on top of them. It was enormous. So large, in fact, that the entire sky was black. The ship was nose-to-nose with the all-but-unarmed Horizon. For this vessel to have appeared to be so small, it must have been hundreds of miles away when first spotted it, which meant that it had traversed the distance in a moment.

"It's some kind of alien of ship. I've never seen anything like this before. It's huge. Please advise."

Split could hear some chatter coming over his communicator while he stood on the deck of the Horizon looking into the eye of the beast. As he looked into what seemed to be the bridge of the vessel, Split could see what appeared to be many eyes, brightly glowing eyes, like those of cats, staring back at him. The creatures were definitely not human, and appeared to be scaly and huge, although it was hard to tell for certain. As for the ship itself, this compartment the Horizon's crew could see into, was toward the belly. Decks extended upward for what appeared to be miles.

From the Command Center, Naziz Kumar chimed in, "I want you to back away slowly. As soon as you have put thirty kilometers between you, turn four degrees south-south west. Head for Azuri Canyon. You should be able to slip in there to find cover, and this ship might not be able to follow."

"You've got it."

Split went to the helm and put the Horizon into reverse. As soon as it started moving away, the alien ship began to rise. Without warning, an energy discharge like a ball of plasma became visible in a compartment at the nose of the vessel.

"Intensify shields!" Split yelled. He could hear muffled shouts coming over the communicator, but it was nothing he could understand.

The energy field engulfing the Horizon grew darker, but it made no difference. The energy ball was released from the alien vessel. It appeared to grow in white hot intensity as it approached the Horizon. The bowling ball-sized energy sphere passed through the Horizon's protective shielding unaffected, like a person walking through a cobweb.

"Retreat! Retreat!" Split could clearly hear in the background coming over his communicator.

The ball hit the center of the deck. The field receiver on the Horizon must have failed because force shield extension was lost. Shards of wood and shrapnel flew every where as the ball went through the ship unhindered. Towne and another crew member were blown clear off the ship plummeting miles down to Sharanda and a crushing death. A third crew member was shredded by the debris from the explosion.

Another energy release. This one caught the deck toward the bow. Shrapnel went every where. The horizon's engines began to whine.

As the ship slowly fell from the sky, Split grabbed the communicator from his sleeve and said, "Deirdre, tell Tina that my last thoughts were of her."

Chapter 24

Third Party Point of View

As usual, Deirdre Lane sat in the Ops Center of Mount Efil. The rest of the staff that usually manned the Center was there as well, minus Gayle Chase, the Empire's director of operations. True to his work ethic, Naziz Kumar was ear-high in books studying the art of war.

Deirdre greatly respected Naziz. He may have been the most diligent man employed by the Empire. Once Argolan had defined his roll in the new era of the Empire, Naziz had started to make it his life's work. This was an exemplary man.

"It's nice to finally have some quiet with all of the commotion of late," Marco Toms said to Lane.

"Sure is," she replied. "Wait. I'm getting an incoming transmission from the Horizon. "

Toms watched as Lane listened intently to her headset. "Done, Split," she said after fidgeting with a few knobs on the shield control display.

Lane turned to Toms and said, "Split asked for shield extension." She then turned from Toms and said, "You're on." The Ops Center's intercom came to life, and Split Jackson's voice filled the room.

"We can see what appears to be a dark spot in the sky. It's too far out to tell what it is." After a brief pause Jackson continued, "It's some kind of alien ship. I've never seen anything like this before. It's huge. Please advise."

The Ops Center, which one minute before had been quite lifeless, suddenly buzzed. Activity was everywhere. Staffers were trying to take telemetric readings of the alien vessel. Simultaneously there were five separate conversations going on.

"How the hell could a ship have approached Sharanda without our radar picking it up?" Lane yelled to Kumar over the chatter.

"I don't know," Kumar yelled back. "Since the Horizon is not a war or diplomatic vessel, and we don't know with what we're dealing, we need to move them to safety." With that he engaged the Ops Center's emergency lights. When the red light came on everyone stopped just as trained.

"I want you to back away slowly. As soon as you have put thirty kilometers between you, turn and head four degrees south-south west. Head for Azuri Canyon. You should be able to slip in there to find cover, and this ship might not be able to follow."

"You've got it," Split responded. Kumar was certain that everyone in the Ops Center could hear the panic in Split's voice.

Just then the door to the Ops Center opened. Gayle Chase entered and sat in her usual place, the command chair. "I'm fully briefed. Can't you get me some video?" she asked, with urgency in her tone of voice, reflecting her understanding of the situation.

"Yeah. I am pirating the image from the Horizon's forward viewer camera," replied Lane.

Everyone in the Ops Center froze. The crew saw an image of a ship the size of a city on the viewer. One could tell from the image on the viewer that the Horizon was pulling away from the vessel. The alien vessel began to climb. A faint glow began to emanate from the belly of its bow.

"Intensify shields!"

The Ops Center came back to life; everybody worked together to one end: Save the Horizon.

Kumar and Chase screamed orders at several people.

"Got it," Kumar cried with glee as the image on the viewer grew hazy from the intensified shielding. The Ops Center crew had just performed a miracle as they had just accomplished the work of minutes in moments.

Unfortunately, it made no difference. The energy, previously clinging benignly to the belly of the alien vessel, was released from the vessel. The viewer's image turned to static.

Over the intercom, the Ops Center crew heard an explosion followed by screams

"Retreat! Retreat!" Chase was now yelling directly to Split. But it was too late. Another explosion could be heard, coupled with the whine of damaged engines attempting to create a lift.

Then Deirdre heard a request that she would take to her grave. "Deirdre, tell Tina that my last thoughts were of her."

The Communications ceased.

Tears streamed down Deirdre's face. The complete complement of the Ops Center crew was numb. The only one who spoke was Kumar, who mumbled to himself, "Shields did nothing. Shields did nothing." Overwhelmed by his incompetence he ran out of the room.

A moment later the alien ship's weapon charged once again. The Ops Center was hit, and all who remained perished.

Chapter 25

The View from the Eye of the Beast

The alien commander sat in his seat watching the ugly planet approach. He had been trapped in this tin can for months traveling to some insignificant planet in a galaxy which was quite far away from home. Trapped without seeing any battle. Trapped without crushing the skull of an adversary under his boot. Now he and his crew would be attacking this species which could, for all intents and purposes, be compared to insects.

He knew this would be no battle. He wanted to stay in his own galaxy, where the battles between good and evil raged on, where quality combat was a part of daily life. But he had a duty. He was compelled to go where the Chan An'ur called him.

And it had called. It had called him before, and now it had called him to this forsaken planet which had outlived its usefulness years ago.

The Chan An'ur was the key component of a weapon with a destructive capability unmatched anywhere in the universe. The Commander's people kept its origin a secret, only a few in the highest levels of their government had access to this information.

The communications officer reported, "Sir, we are in a low orbit around the planet. What are your orders?"

"Have they detected our presence?" the commander asked.

"No. Our shield modulation is allowing full penetration of scans."

In reality the shields did not allow radar readings to "penetrate." This was simply the locution the crew used to describe the duty a specialized computer program performed. The program mapped out any environment where the ship was. It then "projected" a phantom image onto the shields, so the approaching scan appeared to be sensing what was beyond the ship while it was actually sensing the phantom image on the shield. This was not a visual image. It was a collection of data embedded within the shielding to "confuse" the scanning computer, similar to a computer worm. It worked to varying degrees, depending on the scanner's technology, but in this instance, since the technology was so archaic, the phantom image appeared to be believed completely by the enemy's radar.

"Take a full reading of the planet," the commander instructed.

"There are no obvious structures any where on the planet. In fact the only indication of sentient life is a mountain range with a complex shielding system surrounding it and a vessel flying the perimeter of the mountain."

"A vessel?" queried the commander. "This is a space-worthy species, isn't it?"

"Yes. I can't figure out why there is only one vessel. One would expect more."

The alien crew did not realize that Sharanda's radiation field interfered with human propulsion technology, as it had no effect on their technology.

"Bring us down into the atmosphere so that we may see the vessel on the viewer at maximum magnification."

"Aye, sir."

As they did so, the alien vessel moved to within four hundred seventy-five miles of the Horizon.

The alien bridge crew observed six creatures sitting on the deck of their vessel in chairs. Suddenly, one of them stood and pointed an appendage in the general direction of their ship. The commander sighed. This wasn't even going to be interesting.

The commander spoke to his helmsman. "I want an engine burst to bring us to within a kilometer of the vessel. On my mark."

"Yes, sir," replied the helmsman.

"Now"

In an instant the commander's vessel was nose to nose with the Horizon.

"Retract the foreword viewer; I want to look directly into their eyes." The viewer disappeared exposing a window the size of the forward bulkhead.

The commander could see the crew clearly. They were scrawny, pale, sickly looking creatures. There was an obvious commotion arising on the vessel which was followed by a glow that extended from the mountain, engulfing the ship.

"Sir, they have extended the mountain's shielding to encompass the vessel."

"Just hold position and bring forward weapons online." ordered the commander.

The communications officer declared, "Commander, there are communications between the mountain and the ship."

The commander nodded to signify his understanding, never removing his eyes from the ship before him. "Locate the signal's origin within the mountain."

"They're moving, commander," the navigation officer announced. The commander watched as the other ship began to turn away from his.

"Bring her up 1.26 kilometers," ordered the captain.

"The communications between the ship and the mountain are continuing. I think the vessel is taking its orders from an installation within the mountain," the communications officer reported.

The glow of the shields which surrounded the human vessel grew more intense.

"Will our weapon penetrate their shields?"

"It will pass right through, unobstructed," reported the commander's weapons officer.

"Fire!"

As promised the energy orb passed directly through the shields and struck the vessel's deck. Two of the ship's complement were thrown overboard.

"Weapon's online and ready, sir," the weapons officer reported.

"Fire!"

This shot hit the ship squarely, it began to nosedive. The commander smiled. Oh, how he loved combat, challenging or not!

The alien crew watched the Horizon fall, exploding when it hit the ground below. The commander's next order was intended to disable the enemy. "It is logical to assume that the vessel was receiving contact from the Communications Center of this compound. Target this Communications Center."

"Weapons online and ready, sir."

"Fire!"

The crew watched as the energy orb flew to the planet below. It penetrated the shields as if they weren't there. It then cut through the stone façade of the mountain as would a person's hand pass through air. Once the orb arrived at its predetermined coordinates it detonated. An enormous section of Mount Efil's exterior wall separated from the rest of the mountain.

"Engage all batteries and fire!" directed the commander.

More energy orbs descended upon the mountain below like hailstones, each one passing unobstructed through the shields and cutting into the mountain before detonating. Complete sections of the mountain were destroyed.

"This is fun, but playtime is over," thought the commander.

"Weapons Officer, are we going to need to find the power source for the shields, or will our body armor allow us to pass through it?"

"Our personal shielding will allow us to pass through it," replied his weapons officer.

"Good begin landing procedure. Put down within two kilometers of the shield wall. Prepare ground forces for full invasion, and take no prisoners."

Chapter 26

A Dark Meeting

It had been nearly eight months since the envoys of the Oralti Crime Syndicate and the Argalian Trade Empire had met. The crews on the small contingent of Trade Empire ships had been working with renewed vigor since the fire of hope had been rekindled by Kasis Williams' words.

"And remember, he can almost certainly lead us to Masse, which will help you to get your son……who is still alive, by the way………. back."

Kasis had said it as though an afterthought, but this had been the sole focus of Argolan's life since Masse's attack on Mount Efil. It had never really occurred to Argolan that he might be able to retrieve Julian alive. He had only hoped to bring back his son's body for a dignified laying to rest. Argolan knew he could not trust Kasis, but against all better judgment, those words had breathed hope back into the lives of those in the Imperial Armada. Also, for some reason, Argolan sensed that Kasis had told him the truth about Julian.

Finally, now, after these eight long months, Argolan stood at the entry of a long, dark alley in a seedy neighborhood on Sigma One, the appointed meeting place. It was so dark it was difficult to see down to the end of the alley. He could not make out if Zahn and his people were there yet or not.

"Let's go," Argolan said to his party which consisted of Gabriel Williams, Lawrence Young and directors of security from each of their ships.

As the crew walked down the alley, Argolan noted the ground was sticky. Various pieces of random refuse had become attached to the ground making it a little treacherous. This was one of the dirtier worlds Argolan had ever seen.

However, Argolan didn't mind. This was the next step to finding Julian. An enormous amount of time and effort had been invested into this endeavor, and now it was zero hour. In the past eight months, Argolan had inserted himself into the underworld of organized crime in the Sigma System. He had spent resources building credibility within certain circles and making new contacts.

Indeed it had been difficult. In this period Argolan hadn't had any contact with Kasis, but the original point of contact with which Kasis had provided him had proven invaluable. He was well aware that he was fueling his enemies, and possibly Masse himself. Argolan had done things in the past few months with which he was very uncomfortable. He had been in situations and spent time with people which no one of repute should. While he had not broken the law, he had opened himself up to the possibility of having the Empire's licensing rights revoked. It didn't matter. The only thing on his mind was Julian.

At last, a group of dark figures entered the alley. As they came toward Argolan's group he estimated there to be about seven or eight of them. The approaching group stopped its advance. Argolan's stomach dropped. One figure came forward. Argolan reciprocated.

"You're Armish Conklin?" the figure asked.

"Yes." Argolan replied. "Zahn, I presume."

Each man pulled a DNA reader from their pocket. Zahn placed his right index finger on Argolan's reader. Argolan looked at the display which after a moment flashed, "Match" and chirped.

Argolan placed his right index finger on Zahn's reader. As Zahn pulled his device back, Argolan prayed that his alias (which had been quite expensive to reinforce) checked out. While Kasis had actually had Argolan's alias created, Argolan had needed to forge a reputation to bolster the alias, in order to earn the audience with Zahn. Argolan heard Zahn's scanner chirp the affirmative.

Zahn approved and began, "Let's get down to business. You came…"

"Not so fast," Argolan interrupted. "I want visual confirmation. Records can be altered." He knew this from first hand experience.

Argolan pulled his personal notepad from his right pants pocket and touched the display screen. On it appeared a picture of Zahn. Argolan was not going to leave anything to chance. Gabriel advanced from behind Argolan, which resulted in Zahn's men leaping forward and drawing their weapons.

Argolan raised his hands palm forward. "I just need light."

"Stand down," Zahn ordered.

The men retreated.

Gabriel pulled a flashlight from his utility belt and shone it in Zahn's face. Zahn was short and slightly heavy. He had a rather long face which was mostly covered by a thick beard and mustache. He also had a long neck around which was a gold chain holding a vial. He was dressed in black.

"That's good'" Argolan said. Gabriel shut the flashlight off.

"As I was saying you come with very high recommendations. Do you have my money?"

"I'm sorry," was all Argolan responded. That was the phrase, but it was also how Argolan truly felt. "I'm sorry" was the phrase which indicated to Argolan's men that they needed to move in.

Before Zahn's men could react, their guns were taken from them, and they were surrounded by two dozen heavily armed Trade Empire security officers.

"Search them all and bring Zahn before me."

"Yes, Argolan," replied the team lead for the security force. Someone in the crowd winced. After a moment two security men brought Zahn. They forced him to his knees.

"Light," said Argolan. Enough lights came on for Argolan and Zahn to clearly see one another.

Argolan pulled a broken crate out of the corner, turned it over and sat. He looked Zahn in the eye and said, "I am sorry for my deceit, but I must have some information from you. You know what that is."

Zahn began to laugh defiantly and hysterically.

Chapter 27

Some Don't Prosper From a Dark Meeting

As Zahn and his crew walked toward the alley in which he had met so many clients over the years, he noticed an unusually high volume of foot traffic in the surrounding markets. He had come to this alley to meet the likes of Orion Malveaux of the Aldanax Clan, James Masse of the renowned Fifth Fleet, and many high ranking officials of the Guild. Now he would be meeting with Armish Conklin.

Although Zahn was not familiar with Conklin's organization he came with a very high recommendation. He was a newer player in his space but, he paid extremely well. Still, Zahn was a creature of habit, so he took all of the normal "first deal" precautions he normally did, which included rigging the alleyway with a laser sweep which would kill all living things in it in an instant if detonated.

This alley was sort of Zahn's home away from home. He had done many side deals here, deals, which if discovered by the Schuelli Family, would have spelled his demise. They frowned upon side work. Yet what was a man to do? There were jobs out there which needed doing and Zahn was a "doer." With this score Zahn was going to be able to retire. Not bad for a thirty-eight year old.

As Zahn and his six cohorts rounded the corner and turned into the alley, he was abuzz with excitement. This was going to be one of the most lucrative deals of his career. The alley was pitch black. Zahn could make out several silhouettes but could not discern any details.

Zahn's company walked almost to the end of the alleyway and stopped. Zahn waited for a few moments for effect and stepped forward. One of the figures stepped forward to meet him.

"You're Armish Conklin?" Zahn asked.

"Yes," replied the figure. "Zahn, I presume."

Zahn and the figure each pulled out DNA readers and matched their DNA to the other's device.

"Let's get down to business," Zahn began. "You came.."

"Not so fast," the figure cut Zahn off. "I want visual confirmation. Records can be altered."

One of the others leapt forward. Zahn's men stepped forward, drawing and aiming their weapons it.

The figure raised his hands in a posture of surrender, and in an apologetic tone said, "I just need light."

Zahn thought for a moment and told his men to stand down. All of them holstered their weapons. The figure pulled something from its clothing. With a click a light shone brightly in Zahn's face, blinding him.

"That's good," said the figure standing before Zahn. With that the other figure shut off the flashlight, but Zahn was still blinded. He continued anyway.

"As I was saying, you come with very high recommendations. Do you have my money?"

The figure's response to Zahn's question was not what he expected. I'm sorry," the figure said.

"What in the world?" Zahn thought. But before he could finish the thought, the blinded Zahn and his men were surrounded by many heavily armed men.

"Search them and bring Zahn before me," the figure ordered.

"Yes, Argolan," was the response Zahn heard. He winced. If he had only taken the precaution of inspecting the figure visually, he would have recognized him. Unfortunately Argolan, or rather Armish, had come with a personal reference from one of Zahn's most trusted business allies. Now he was in grave trouble because of this oversight.

Zahn had no personal feelings toward Argolan one way or the other, but one of his main clients, James Masse had it in for the man. Zahn had recently supplied Masse with falsified evidence incriminating Argolan. This was bad.

Two men came over to Zahn and patted him down. After removing his primary and backup weapons, they brought Zahn to Argolan, forcing him down onto his knees.

"Light!" Argolan instructed. He approached Zahn and said, "I am sorry for my deceit, but I must have some information from you. You know what it is."

As the light came on Zahn could see that many of the people who had been in the marketplace minutes before were now holding him and his men captive.

Zahn laughed.

And laughed.

And laughed.

As soon as his hands were free, he would detonate the laser sweep, and all in the alley would die, including Argolan. Funny that he would be finishing Masse's job for him.

Argolan proceeded. "I have no interest in you. All I want is my son. To get him I am going to need your help."

Argolan paused and waited, but Zahn said nothing. Zahn knew that Argolan was a God-fearing man. He was weak. He would never have the courage to do what he would need to do to extract the information from Zahn. Besides, Zahn would never give up Masse. The man was dangerous and had the backing of the Guild, an insurmountable combination.

Argolan piped up again. "Please understand that I will do anything that I must to get him back. There is a man named Kasis Williams who is a member of the Oralti Crime Syndicate who wants you." Zahn looked down. Argolan Continued, "I am reasonably certain that he will kill you after he gets the information he wants from you. I am prepared to turn you over to him if it comes to that, but I would really rather not."

Zahn could see that that caught the attention of the figure that had held the light on Zahn and his men. He approached Argolan and whispered something in his ear which Zahn couldn't make out.

"Please trust me, Gabriel," was Argolan's response. He then turned back to Zahn.

"I promise to let you go unmolested. I know you set me up, but I can forgive that. Please just help me find my boy."

Then Argolan said something else Zahn hadn't expected.

"Do you have children?" Argolan asked.

Zahn thought about his two wonderful sons who were eight and ten years old, but he didn't respond.

"We've been seeking you for months. We know all about you. I know you have two boys. Put yourself in my shoes. Imagine if one of them were taken from you. Imagine the pain it would cause you. Please help me, and I promise to take you and your family into my protection."

The man's arrogance incensed Zahn.

"Take me under your protection? Do you know who I am?" Zahn tugged his left arm away from the man who was holding it and reached to his belt where he kept the laser sweep's detonator. He grabbed the detonator and pushed the button…

Chapter 28

The Perfidious One

Nothing happened. Argolan observed Zahn has he pressed a switching mechanism again and again.

It was Argolan's turn to cackle. "If you're trying to detonate your laser sweep, well, my men are great at finding and dismantling things."

Pursing his lips, Argolan paced contemplatively back and forth in front of Zahn. "Look, there is no reason any of us has to die here tonight. I will take you and your family into the Empire or do anything necessary to protect you from Masse. Please, just help me, and then we can all see our families again. Won't you please do that?" Zahn was broken. He could empathize with Argolan's feelings. How he dearly loved his boys! And interestingly enough, in the world from which he came, Zahn was not used to being treated like this. Argolan honestly appeared to want to walk away and seemed to truly want him to benefit as well.

In Zahn's world people were disposable. If one needed information from someone, one tortured him until he broke, and everyone broke. Argolan genuinely seemed to not want to go that route. He had a caring and compassionate demeanor about him. Zahn knew that just coming to him had been a sheer act of desperation on Argolan's part, and Zahn now decided that he would like to help.

"All right, Argolan but you have to promise to take me and my family under Imperial protection."

"You have my word."

Zahn collected his thoughts for a moment and then began.

"Masse has plans for the Empire. He is working somewhat in alignment with the Guild to—"

An enormous commotion erupted at the end of the alleyway as hundreds of armed men swarmed in. The Empire's security contingent was disarmed, and everyone was lined up against the alley's side wall. That is, everyone except Zahn.

A hush fell over the group as a figure walked down the alley. Before the figure reached Zahn, Argolan could see that it was Kasis. Argolan started to take a step toward Kasis, only to meet with the barrel of a laser rifle.

"Kasis," Argolan shouted to be heard, "Zahn was just telling us where Julian is being held. Please let him continue."

Kasis reached Zahn, stopped, pulled a laser pistol out of his jacket pocket, aimed it at Zahn's head and pulled the trigger.

"Why would you do this?" a horrified Argolan asked. Now how would he find Julian?

Without glancing at Argolan, Kasis placed his right foot on Zahn's lifeless chest and reached down with his right hand. He grabbed the chain holding the vial around Zahn's neck and ripped it away from him.

Kasis turned to Argolan and said, "Thank you. You have done in just eight months what my organization has not been able to do in years." Argolan sprang toward Kasis, only to be met with gun barrels again.

Lawrence Young slowly moved to Argolan to console him, while Gabriel started on Kasis.

"Uncle Kasis, how could you do this? You know Zahn was our only chance for Julian's return. How could you kill him in cold blood like that?"

Kasis smiled. "Do you think that your parents left Sigma because mob life was neat and clean? One does what one has to, Little One. But your concern for that man! You really remind me of your father."

"My father was right about you!" Gabriel fumed.

Kasis pulled an electronic journal out of the same coat pocket from which he had drawn his gun. He extended it to Argolan who took it. "In this journal you will find everything you need, Masse's location, his hideout's schematics and blueprints, his planetary defenses. I wish you luck in recovering Julian." Kasis turned his head to look at Gabriel. "I'm sorry things had to play themselves out like this. I know you have some….disdain for my lifestyle, but I do hope that at some point in the future, we may develop a relationship."

Kasis gave one of his flamboyant hand signals, and the group departed the alley leaving only Zahn's and the Empire's people.

"Please go," Argolan instructed Zahn's men, who looked skeptical but slowly complied.

"Let's get back to our fleet. I would like to turn in. I've been used more than enough for one day."

Chapter 29

Kumar's Transmission

The group's shuttle was near the flagship when the communications computer chirped. As Young pressed a button on the console, Drake Stetson, Argolan's assistant manager on the flagship, came into view on the monitor. He had a grave look on his face.

"Lawrence, please ask Argolan to come and see me the moment you arrive back on the flagship."

Young looked back at Argolan who was studying the information in the journal with unmatched attention.

Young turned back to the monitor and queried, "Are you all right, Drake?"

Stetson let out a slow, deliberate sigh.

"I don't mean to be brash, but please just deliver the message to Argolan."

"Will do," Young said.

The screen went dark, and Young was left with a feeling of foreboding. He looked over at Argolan, hesitant to interrupt but decided that the urgency in Stetson's voice indicated this warranted the interruption.

"Argolan."

Argolan looked up. Young's face must have been displaying his feelings because Argolan put the journal down.

"What's wrong, Lawrence?"

Young thought for a moment. "I don't know. Drake just sent a communication asking me to have you see him immediately upon arriving at the flagship."

"That's not unusual. We've been in Deep Space for quite a while, and any one of a number of circumstances could have come up demanding my presence. I wouldn't worry."

Young continued to reflect and finally replied, "No, it's more than that. Something was definitely troubling Drake. I just don't know what."

"Well, we'll find out soon enough," Argolan said, pointing at the front view screen as the flagship drew close.

The shuttle landed, and Argolan asked everyone to remain aboard the flagship in case they were needed. Young had been with him for a long time, and Argolan had learned that it was usually unwise to ignore Young's intuition. If a situation were brewing, it might be convenient to have both Young and Williams on board the flagship.

"Why don't all of you head down to the restaurant? I would like to buy all of you dinner in celebration of our success on Sigma."

The party agreed, but as they were leaving, Young looked back at Argolan. He was deeply concerned.

While heading to the bridge, Argolan noted what appeared to be an exceedingly somber tone among the staff. He went straight to Stetson who sat in the command chair when he arrived. He didn't look well at all.

When Stetson saw Argolan he stood up and said, "Argolan, please sit."

Although it was unusual for Argolan to follow any suggestion without questioning it, he complied. There was something about Stetson's demeanor which caused Argolan alarm.

While Argolan sat, Stetson pressed several buttons on the armrest of the command chair, and Naziz Kumar appeared on the forward viewer with his image paused.

"We received this message via low band width messaging a little while ago." Stetson hit another button, and Kumar's image jumped to life. The video was unusually grainy, most likely partially due to the low band width over which the message was sent coupled with the distance, but even that wouldn't account for this level of distortion.

Kumar began. "Argolan and Trade Empire fleet: Approximately fourteen hours ago an unidentifiable alien vessel entered Sharanda's airspace and attacked the Horizon. All hands were lost. Subsequently the vessel turned its weapons on Mount Efil. It hit the Ops Center, where I should have been….." Kumar's voice drifted off.

"All in the Ops Center were killed, Deirdre, Marco, Stan, Arthur, Madeline and everyone else. The vessel's weapons penetrated the shields and walls of Mount Efil as though they weren't even there. Then a ground assault, such as we have never seen, began. The armor that the attackers wore allowed them to pass through our shields unhindered. They moved with unimaginable speed. They killed everyone and destroyed the entire facility. Only about five hundred of our ships were able to escape with perhaps forty thousand employees."

Stetson had already seen the message; he spent this time observing Argolan. He was clearly shaken already, but Stetson could tell the news of the death toll really impacted him. However, as all great leaders do in a time of crisis, Argolan kept up a strong front.

"Mount Efil is crushed. All of the weaponry stocks we have built up are destroyed, and most of our operations employees have perished," Naziz paused once again. "I believe that we have been able to evade pursuit. We have brought the fleet into the Norson Expanse just off of the Blanner Black Hole and used negative gravity shielding to mask our signature from detection. We believe that their "eyes" have not able to detect us because of this. However, the debris has damaged some of our vessels.

"We have set a course for the fleet to the coordinates sub-layered under this message. Use encryption key 15alphabravobravo3164 to decode. The key will be valid for twenty-eight days. We will arrive at the rendezvous point in nineteen days. I will do my best to hold the fleet together for three months. There will be no way I can keep it together for longer than that, as we only have fuel and supplies for about that long. If in three months I have not received word from you, I will assume that circumstances are not good and disperse the fleet across the Galaxy. God speed."

The transmission ended.

Stetson observed Argolan, who didn't miss a beat. "Drake, get a video communications port open to our little fleet and have someone go get my party from the restaurant. I'll be back in ten minutes at which time I would like to meet them here."

Chapter 30

Argolan's Transmission

Argolan sat on the edge of his bed in his personal quarters. So much had happened in these past months that he was emotionally drained; in fact, he felt depleted. Normally in the past, when Argolan had felt depleted, he was able to have a good rest or take a vacation and come back to his life with a new perspective. This was different. Times were different. He might never have that opportunity again.

Everything which Argolan had worked to build over the past thirty-nine years had been destroyed in the last eight months. Everything. However, he wasn't going to let this defeat him. He remembered how he had pitied Masse at Angel's funeral, and he remembered his promise to the Lord to never let that happen to him.

He prayed, "Heavenly Father, I need you more now possibly than I ever have before. Please give me strength and let Thy Spirit be with me when I deliver this message to my people. Please also keep my vision clear. I ask for these things humbly in the name of Jesus Christ. Amen."

Argolan walked over to the sink and splashed cold water on his face before heading back to the bridge. Upon arrival, Argolan entered slowly. He could tell by Gabriel's and Lawrence's faces that they already knew. Young came up to him and gave him a strong hug of reinforcement, which Argolan appreciated. He knew that even through such tumultuous times, Lawrence would stand by him.

"Open the com port, please."

The view screen came to life with little boxes, each box depicting the bridge of one of the fleet's ships. He could see all of his friends, that is, the ones whom he hadn't left behind to be slaughtered.

"Audio communication is fleet-wide in addition to the video of the bridges," Stetson reported to Argolan.

"Thank you. There is no soft way to deliver this news. Sharanda has fallen. It was attacked by an alien force. Mount Efil, our home, is destroyed. Well over half of the staff and almost three-quarters of the fleet was destroyed in the attack. After we retrieve Julian, we will be going to meet with the remainder of the fleet."

"I'm sorry I have…" Argolan fought back tears. "…let all of you down. I promise you that we will emerge stronger from this. I won't let it be any other way."

Argolan pushed the button to end communication, and the screen went black.

Chapter 31

Abandoned

Masse was bored of his new toy. It cried in pain and it ate, but it wouldn't talk. Julian Paul had said not one word the entire time Masse had held him captive on Eden. Masse reached the door to Julian's quarters, the guards parted to let him in. When he went in, Julian was lying in a corner of the room on the floor. He didn't even glance at Masse. Julian was badly disfigured due to the torture he had been put through by Masse. Perhaps that was why he didn't look at him.

"I left plenty of routes for your father to come to find you. His logical course would have been to go to the crime syndicates where the evidence that was manufactured against him was generated. I sent word to all of the bosses that I was holding you here alive, but nothing. I even have the head of the Oralti Crime Syndicate, a man named Kasis, on my payroll. I gave him disinformation about our little paradise here in the hopes that Argolan would come, but nothing. In fact, that faulty intelligence was to lead your father into a trap and to certain doom when he arrived."

Kasis was indeed on Masse's payroll. He had supplied Argolan with the data journal that Masse had given him. However, he had not informed Masse that Argolan was coming. If the Guild took control of the Sigma System, it would spell the end of the crime syndicates and general commerce in the system. Kasis would never allow that.

Unfortunately, where there is freedom, some will abuse it and run businesses that cater to the darker side of human existence.

"I did hear, however, that one of my old sources, indeed the very one who supplied me with those falsified documents, turned up dead. It appears, though, that this was only a case of syndicate rivalry. Your father is not coming for you.

"Just look at yourself. You're a menace. You're hideous. I wouldn't come for you either.

"Mr. Paul, we tortured you for the first three months you were here, but you wouldn't offer us any information. Since you are no longer of any value to me, I am going to have you killed one week from today. No torture, just death. If you find your power of speech in the meantime, perhaps I'll reconsider."

He left the room without Julian so much as glancing at him.

Masse had tried everything in the past few months to get Paul to speak. He had even offered him lordship over a star system, but Julian never said a word. Now it finally appeared that it would all be over for Julian.

Julian knew that there was a good reason that Argolan had not come for him. He knew that Argolan would have done anything to get him back. Perhaps he hadn't survived Masse's attack on Sharanda.

Chapter 32

The Plan

The Empire's mini-fleet hid behind the No'on star as it observed Eden. It was somewhat reminiscent of Old Earth being comprised of mostly water with a few significant land masses. However, these land masses were undeveloped.

For the past three weeks they had observed Eden, but hadn't learned anything valuable from the endeavor. Argolan had studied the data journal he had obtained from Kasis. It contained incredibly, in fact, suspiciously detailed information about Eden, Masse's fortress and even the location where Julian was being held. Nonetheless, suspicious or not, this data journal was Argolan's best chance to get Julian back.

The fortress itself didn't look as though it was going to be a problem to move through. However, penetrating it would be a challenge. Argolan's organization was expert in ground and space salvage, but not water. Moving effectively and undetected through water is an art unto itself. There are sub-aquatic salvage experts. Unfortunately, neither Argolan nor any his staff was one of them. That expertise had never been called for within the Empire.

Then, something on the screen at which Argolan stared, stood out to him. There was a pre-construction entry indicating a tunnel. The tunnel ran from the base of a mountain on a land mass approximately forty miles east of the fortress, under the sea floor to directly beneath the belly chamber of the fortress. If the crew wanted to avoid a toe-to-

toe slugging match with the Fifth Fleet, this was their path. Of course, it would be closely monitored and probably even laden with traps, but this was still the best option.

Chapter 33

Help on the Way

Lyle Nole was on the monitor in Masse's quarters delivering the good news. Masse could barely contain himself. In fact, the Admiral was so excited that he ran down to the quarters where Julian Paul was being held to share the good news with him. As the guards parted, Masse all but sprinted into the room.

"Oh, do I have some good news for you," he paused for effect. "Your execution is postponed, as Argolan is on his way here. Quite frankly, I am astounded he was stupid enough to fall for that data journal. He is a coward, a cheat, etcetera, but he is not stupid. I planted that journal with my contact in the Oralti Crime Syndicate, and it contains a map of this compound on it. Of course the map is altered. Instead of leading them to you, it will lead them into a dive acclimatization chamber which, once they are in, will lock and fill with water. You could say that your father is going to walk right into a trap." Masse chuckled at his double entendre.

Julian, who was crumpled on the floor in the corner as always, attempted to stand but couldn't.

"Hmm," Masse said intrigued by Paul's theatrics.

"You'll never get him," Julian spat out at little more than a whisper. Three months of daily torture had really taken its toll on him.

Masse chortled, "Time will tell. Time will tell."

And Masse walked out.

Chapter 34

On the Doorstep

It had taken two weeks of hiking, but Argolan and his company of fifteen were finally below the lower level entry room of Masse's fortress. No traps, no detected surveillance devices. It had been too easy, almost as though Argolan had been directed to this point by neon signs.

It hadn't really been easy. The company had been dropped off by shuttle on the far side of a land mass about forty miles east of the underground tunnel's entrance.

Hoping to avoid being detected by radar, Argolan and company decided to wait for a weather event which could mask their arrival. Fortunately, a hail storm developed just off of the east coast of the land mass. That would actually be the ideal cover as the fist-sized hail stones would clutter radar. Unfortunately, it had caused the shuttle landing to be very difficult. After landing the shuttle, the group had to walk through a forest, over a mountain, and after the mountain, of course, was the tunnel.

As the team looked up at the hatch leading into the fortress, Argolan glanced first at Lawrence Young, then at Gabriel Williams. They were with him as they had been throughout the entire endeavor of attempting to retrieve Julian.

"Would you two please come with me?" he asked them. Young and Williams, a little confused, complied and followed Argolan off into a niche in the rock wall of the tunnel.

"I just wanted to thank you and tell you how much your support and help has meant to me. Gabriel, I thank you for your loyal friendship to Julian." Gabriel looked a bit embarrassed.

Argolan turned to Young and looked him straight in the eyes. Putting his right hand on Young's left shoulder he said, "We've been together for a long time, my friend." Young nodded in agreement. "It's not likely that we are going to survive this. I know how you feel about Julian; you've never made it a secret, and I know you're here to support me and I love you for it." A tear came to Argolan's eye. He reached forward and the two men embraced.

"Are you two ready?"

Williams and Young looked at each other, and turning back to Argolan, Young said, "We would follow you anywhere, Sir. We're ready."

The three men returned to the group.

Argolan observed Dan Small giving preparatory instructions to the rest of the crew. He had strong leadership potential. After observing Dan in action for a couple of minutes, Argolan stopped watching and stepped in front of his men.

"I know that you have all volunteered to be here, and I thank you. All of you are like family to me, I want you to know that. Now let's go get Julian!"

The group relayed like feelings toward Argolan.

Abraham Kalman came forth with his Chemical Chisel, and before the company knew it, they were looking up into Masse's fortress.

Chapter 35

A Nice Day

Watching Argolan's company on his monitor, Masse couldn't help but laugh. Argolan had not detected the cameras, and he was walking into an obvious ambush. "How did this man ever build such success?" Masse wondered. Perhaps Argolan wasn't as smart as Masse had always deemed him to be.

Masse hit a button on his computer console, and Lyle Nole's face appeared on the screen.

"I want a group of SEALs at my quarters in five minutes to accompany me to the observation room above the dive acclimatization chamber. I believe that there is going to be a great show to watch."

"Yes, Sir!" Nole replied with a salute. The screen went black.

The observation room was located directly above the acclimatization chamber, separated by a glass partition. The observation room had been installed for training purposes so that current SEALs could get dive-acclimated while cadets could observe the process from above. It worked quite well. The failure rate for seals about to go through this portion of their training for the first time was about twenty-three percent; these cadets became too frightened to go through with the process. In the Fifth Fleet it was almost zero percent. The cadets watched this exercise first-hand dozens of times before actually doing it themselves.

Masse was buzzed with excitement and thought about his thirty years of work which was about to bear fruit. It was almost electrifying.

Masse considered bringing Julian in to watch in order to taunt him, but Masse wanted to stay focused. It was not Paul that he was ultimately after but Argolan.

Masse got up and exited his quarters to await his SEALs. This was shaping up to be a nice day.

Chapter 36

Vacuity

At his insistence, Lawrence Young climbed the force ladder first. After looking around the fortress's lower chamber, for a moment, he called down, "all clear." The security contingent went next followed by Gabriel and ultimately Argolan. He wondered how they had gone undetected in the tunnels. The tunnels were a secret, not on public record anywhere, but could Masse's ego be so big, could he feel so untouchable, that he didn't even bother to monitor that route into his fortress? Argolan doubted it. It was more likely that they were walking into a trap.

In a half-squatting position, Young led the security men and the rest of the company to the exit from the room. Argolan came to the front of the group and referred to the electronic journal.

"Lawrence, we're going to head north for fifteen meters, we will then turn west. At the end of that hallway there will be a ceiling hatch with a ladder which extends to, actually beyond, the level on which Julian is being held."

They made it to the hatch without seeing anyone. Argolan could sense that something was clearly wrong. How could they not have been detected? How could they have stumbled on no one?

Before opening the hatch Young looked at Argolan.

"We are definitely walking into a trap."

"I know, but what option do we have? This is going to be our only opportunity. We can bring our whole fleet here, and it won't be able to have even a fighting chance against the Fifth Fleet. Besides, this trap may offer us our best chance. We are clearly being granted some ground for which we would probably have had to fight were it not for the trap. We *must* see this through." Young nodded in agreement, opened the hatch, and climbed the ladder. His head poked through the deck to the level above.

"All clear," he chuckled. He chuckled not because he was amused but because he was incredulous. This Masse was a fool. He decidedly could have crushed the Assault Team even before it entered his fortress, yet apparently he wanted to play some kind of game with them. Well, Young was not going to let him win.

The rest of the group ascended the ladder and joined Young. Once again, Argolan referred to the journal. Argolan had memorized every detail it contained but he would not leave anything, even mental failure, to chance. He used the miniature computer as a means to validate his memory. Argolan pointed in the direction they should take. The company continued to move stealthily through the hallways encountering no one.

Argolan returned to the head of the group and addressed Young once again. "Continue to travel straight ahead for approximately one hundred thirty more meters. There will be chambers to the left and to the right. To the right is a dive acclimatization chamber, a dead end. To the left is a sub-aquatic testing chamber. We will cut through there. On the far end of that chamber is a door which will take us to one last hallway, leading directly to Julian's room. We are going to need to be ready for a fight, as his chamber will definitely be guarded."

"Does everyone hear that?" asked Young. "We are going to take a left into a chamber up ahead. Once through that chamber we will be within view of Julian's quarters which will be guarded. Expect resistance."

All responded: Understood.

"Before we continue, I think we should offer a prayer." Everyone knelt and Argolan began, "Heavenly Father, we realize the danger in which we find ourselves as we endeavor to save our brother, Julian. We ask that you would offer us protection in this perilous position and quicken our minds that we will be able to meet the dangers we are about to face in the best possible way. If any of us are to perish, please allow it to be quick and dignified. We ask for these things in the name of Jesus Christ. Amen."

After a collective, "Amen," the group stood and began to move. As they inched down the hallway, there was still no one to be seen. The curious vacuity continued even as they reached the sub-aquatic testing chamber. They stopped and leaned with backs against the wall on the side of the chamber. Young peered around the corner expecting to see a room full of SEALs, but he saw nothing, no one. Gun drawn he carefully rounded the corner and moved silently into the room. Argolan, who now had his own laser pistol drawn, was nervous as he watched his friend disappear to where the trap was most likely to be sprung. However, after a few seconds, Young's hand popped out of the room and signaled the group to follow.

Argolan entered the chamber, which was fairly large. He took note of a cage similar to the one used by Kalman in which he took advantage of the energy grapplers to examine the chest the Focus had found. There was also a launch well. Launch wells were a round hole in the floor which opened directly into the ocean. This specific launch well was approximately twenty feet in diameter.

Suddenly something was wrong. The floor shifted, the door slammed shut behind them, and the room began to fill with water.

Chapter 37

Fish in a Bowl

Masse's group waited and watched the dive acclimatization chamber from the observation room above. His most-favored Senior Chief Petty Officer, Orff Stanlin, had been full of questions that day.

"Sir, why would Argolan and company attempt to reach Paul via the dive acclimatization chamber? It's a dead end!"

"I fed him some disinformation which will lead him there. We were able to get him an architectural layout of this facility. In that blueprint, the sub-aquatic testing chamber and the dive acclimatization chambers were reversed."

"Sir, permission to speak frankly?" asked Stanlin.

Stanlin's candor was part of what Masse appreciated about him. That, and he was a killing machine with fierce loyalty and honor, a trait which Masse remembered himself as having once possessed. Stanlin strongly reminded Masse of himself when he was younger.

"Of course."

"I am not feeling good about this kill. It is without honor. They are going to be trapped like fish in a bowl."

"I can appreciate that. Your sense of honor and duty are two of the greatest reasons that I hold you in such high regard. However, this order comes from directly from Guild leadership. The Naval brass is no longer running the show. When we have some time, I will explain the Galactic power/political structure of the military, the Guild, and business. You'll understand better then. For now all we need to know is that Argolan is persona non grata, and carry out our orders."

Masse had now lied to his young protégé, someone to whom he had promised himself he would never lie. The Guild had not authorized Argolan's death. In fact, this would probably infuriate "CORE Leadership", but what did it matter? This act was to be the book end on Masse's life. Of course Masse wouldn't die today, but this was to be the last significant act of his life. All that he had done for the past quarter-plus century had been geared toward reaching this moment. HIS moment.

An update on the intruders' position came over Masse's earpiece.

"Prepare to watch the show, everyone, they're coming."

He tingled with excitement.

Chapter 38

Retrieval, Hero Worship and Dinner

Kasis Williams sat down to dinner with his wife and children for the first time in many weeks. Directly after meeting up with Argolan, his team, and Zahn on Sigma One, Williams had had an errand to run which took him outside of the Sigma System. Oh, how he had longed to see his family again. His wife, Dorothy, who was actively involved in his career, asked Kasis an obvious "yes question." "You retrieved it?"

"Oh, yes. Took it right from around the neck of his corpse." Kasis chuckled, "and I may have even thwarted Masse's plans while in the process! Not only did I retrieve the vial, but I downloaded the corrected schematic for Masse's fortress into the data pad he gave me before giving it to Argolan. This should enable Argolan the chance to avert Masse's ambush, or at least give him a remote chance of surviving. I hope Argolan kills that man."

Williams' children took no special interest in the content of this conversation, as conversations like this took place over dinner all of the time in their household.

Of course the blueprints for Masse's fortress were not public record. They were kept quite safely only in Masse's personal vault and on file in the Master Architect's firm archives, located within the Sigma Commerce Bureau's classified documents vault. Luckily, Kasis had high-level connections at the Architect's firm. The price that Kasis had been required to pay for the layout had been astronomical, but it would be worth every penny if it could help to pull off this most brilliant double cross.

"Was he everything that you had anticipated?"

"All and more. I made it very difficult for him, and he rose to the occasion. I hope that he retrieves his boy in good condition, and we have the chance to meet again."

Dorothy watched as Kasis glowed with the memory of having met his hero.

Kasis stared back at the love of his life and returned to their original topic. "Perhaps history will look back at me, and instead of remembering me as a criminal, will remember me as the man who helped Argolan to take down the menace, Masse!"

Williams and his wife laughed heartily.

Chapter 39

Shockwaves

As Masse prepared for the greatest moment of his life, he received a disturbing communication in his earpiece.

"Admiral, I am afraid that Argolan and company turned into the sub-aquatic testing chamber instead of the dive acclimatization chamber," reported Lyle Nole.

"Why would he do that?" asked the now-irate Masse.

No answer ever came.

A tectonic shockwave hit the fortress, which buckled in response. There had recently been many of these waves due to subterranean plate shifting, but this one was the worst to date. Masse could sense a direction change in the air current within the fortress. This indicated a breach of the fortress' hull.

As the group of observers looked down to the level below, they could see a steady stream of water running into it. Masse called down to the Central Command Center (CentCom) of the fortress via his earpiece, but there was no response. Apparently communications were down. Another shockwave hit the facility, throwing everyone in the room off balance.

Knowing that Argolan and company would be drowned while returning to the underground caverns, Masse instantly decided to return to CentCom and allow the sea to deal with Argolan. "Come with me!" he ordered his company while already running toward the Command Center.

149

Chapter 40

The Bond

A second shift of the room occurred, and this time Argolan's band was knocked to the floor, soaking all of them. A horrid screech, like that of heavy metal scraping against a rock under the water, could be heard throughout the chamber.

"We need to move quickly!" Argolan encouraged the crew. With Argolan now at point, the group went to the far end of the Testing Chamber. Argolan threw open the hatch. The guards who normally watched Julian's room had run off with the first shockwave and were nowhere to be seen.

Argolan and troop ran down to Julian's quarters. Dan Small scurried to the front and used a DNA mimicry sensor to scan the DNA reader on the wall.

"Dan, please do this quickly," Young urged.

The sensor beeped, and Kalman placed his hand on the scanner. It scanned, and the door opened. Argolan rushed in followed by Young, Gabriel Williams and a few of the security men.

Julian was crumpled in the corner on the floor.

"Julian!" Argolan screamed at the motionless form.

Young saw the panic and pain on Argolan's face as he rushed over to his inert son.

Argolan knelt beside Julian's face-down body, rolled him over so that they were face-to-face and cradled Julian's head and shoulders in his lap. All could see that Julian was badly disfigured. His arms had obviously been broken and had healed improperly.

Argolan was sobbing. "Oh, my wonderful boy! What has that madman done to you in the name of avenging himself upon me?" He held Julian tightly.

"Father, you were right about my strength," Julian labored to speak, he was whispering barely audibly. "I told him nothing!"

"I've always seen that strength. It never occurred to me that you would betray the Empire. But even if you had, I would still love you."

"Fa… Ahh… Father, I know where I've seen the chest before that the Fo…the Focus was carryin…" Julian lost consciousness.

Young, who never had children himself, was moved by the exchange between father and son. And all of a sudden he understood. He understood why Julian had always taken such a prominent role in Argolan's life, why their relationship had become more important to Argolan than anything, including his relationship with Young. Undeniably, there was a bond of nurturing and strengthening of manhood that occurred in the relationship between a father and son. While Young realized that no one who wasn't a father could completely appreciate this bond, he had just gotten a glimpse into it.

Young had always planned on having a family. Unfortunately due to the *focus* he had placed on his career with the Trade Empire, it had never happened. His career had become his wife and children. He was old now, in the dusk of his life. Nonetheless, this was an endeavor which Young now decided he must pursue.

Argolan lifted Julian up onto his right shoulder and exited the room. The others followed.

Chapter 41

Another Escape

As the assault team was retreating, another shockwave hit. Again screeching sounds, indicative of a hull breach, could be heard. It became apparent to the crew just how severe the damage to the facility was becoming. Clearly, the structural soundness of the fortress was being undermined. Now the group passed frantic people in the hallway, but no one paid attention to them. Sailors scrambled to get to their emergency stations to lock down problems.

As the Empire's band arrived at the hatch to the lower level, Argolan reached into his pocket and pulled out the journal. Gabriel couldn't believe the physical prowess Argolan was displaying carrying Julian on his shoulder with one hand while at the same time reaching into his pocket with the other. Argolan was not a young man!

After studying the journal for a moment, Argolan pointed and said, "We need to go that way."

While all were thinking it, Young, the most outspoken of the group, was the first to say it. "Argolan, we came from down below. Don't we need to go back that way?"

"We can't. Assuming that the lower level is not filled with water and is able to accommodate us, we would be targets in the tunnels during our escape. All Masse's men would have to do is direct some of this water down there, and we would be drowned. Or if the fortress's structure is compromised severely enough, all of the water which is taken on will rush to the lowest point, directing it into the tunnels. We must escape on a ship."

The team reached the landing bay. There, to Argolan's surprise and delectation, as if by providence, the Soulseeker awaited them, unguarded.

"Dan, I want you to use that computer," Argolan pointed to a computer terminal near the entrance to the landing bay. "See if you can break into the fortresses's computer system. Locate the launch corridor override protocols. Execute a script to run the program, opening a launch window. Everyone else, into the Soulseeker! Gabriel, please take your friend from me."

Gabriel smiled and grabbed the now conscious Julian from Argolan and took him onboard the shuttle. Argolan stayed behind to cover Dan Small.

After a couple of minutes, Small finished, and the two men went to the Soulseeker. Small, who loved to talk, began chatting with Argolan. "Masse must really have been confident of the impenetrability of this fortress. He has only very low-level encryption on his systems. This was a very easy job. He real-"

Small stopped when Argolan's left hand rested on his right shoulder. When Small turned to face Argolan, Argolan was laughing.

"No, my old friend," Argolan said, "You won't get me that easily."

Turning to Small, Argolan said, "I want you to verify your work on the other computer terminal we passed back in the hallway, NOT on any of the landing bay terminals. Do you understand me?"

"Yes, Argolan," Small replied. He turned around and headed to the door. Argolan followed.

Small worked for a few minutes while an impatient Argolan stood watch.

"Please hurry," Argolan urged Small.

"I don't believe it. Your intuition was right. It was a dummy program I hacked into, a program designed to make me think I had issued a command to open the corridor's window. But in actuality we would have been trapped in an unopened launch corridor."

Small worked for another minute pushing buttons. "Got it. This time I'm sure of it."

Had it not been for the commotion and disarray within the fortress, this delay would have been sufficient time for Masse and his men to lay siege on the assault team. But Masse's men were busy trying to win another battle; the battle of maintaining the structure of the fortress.

Argolan and Small ran onto the shuttle, and the hatch closed behind them. The Soulseeker lifted off and began to head for the fleet.

Chapter 42

Pursue!

Masse sat in his CentCom command chair giving orders to his different teams regarding how best to best maintain the fortress' structural integrity.

"Admiral, we are receiving reports of a vessel launching from Corridor 6J2XA. It's the Soulseeker," His communications officer interrupted. "Do you want us to open fire?"

"No! I must have that ship back!" Masse yelled as the Monster came unleashed. It was about to massacre the whole incompetent crew in Central Command as another shockwave came in. This one was so strong it dwarfed the others. New sections of the fortress crumbled, while at the same time, sections that were being repaired from earlier damage were destroyed. The fortress began to take on massive amounts of water. Masse was able to force the Monster back into the shadows for now.

"All hands, abandon the fortress! Prepare the Fleet to pursue the Imperial Armada!"

Chapter 43

Reunion

The Soulseeker had dropped the rest of the members of the assault team off on their respective ships and was now heading back to the Liahona with Julian, Gabriel and the small security contingent from the Liahona. The three days of travel back to the Liahona had given Julian some time to rest and recuperate somewhat. He was still very weak and traumatized, but he was showing some definite signs of improvement, partly due to the nutrition he had received since being rescued.

Gabriel slowly approached the bunk on which Julian rested, not wanting to disturb him. As Gabriel neared Julian, he thought better of the approach and turned to walk away.

"So now you won't even talk to me?" came Julian's voice from behind Gabriel. Gabriel smiled as he turned around.

"I just didn't want to disturb you," he replied. "It was pretty rough, huh?"

"The torture was bad. I don't know how I managed, I just did. But as bad as that was, the worst part was being close to Masse. I could look into his eyes and see he has no soul. It is pure hatred. He's dangerous. There are no limits on what he's capable of."

The two men sat in companionable silence for a few moments, before Julian, smiling, continued, "So I see you have finally gotten a ship of your own!"

That warmth of that smile melted Gabriel. "The ship's prior commander went AWOL! It hasn't been the same without you. There has been a hole on this ship in your absence."

"I thought about you many times during my captivity on Eden. I thought about you, and your parents, and your family's history in the Sigma System. I know you are avidly opposed to violence, probably because you want to stay as far away from anything resembling mob life as possible. But I'm telling you that this man must be stopped, or he is going to bring the full might of the Fifth Fleet to bear on the Trade Empire."

Julian could tell he had clearly gotten to Gabriel, but said nothing more. For now it was probably better just to leave the subject alone. Even though Gabriel had some kind of a blind spot when it came to this type of issue, Julian knew that the reality was the reality. The Serpent would never rest until it had killed its prey.

The Soulseeker put down on the Liahona, and all on board departed, with Julian going in one direction and Gabriel in another.

When Gabriel realized that Julian was not following him, he turned around and yelled back. "Julian, you need to go to the infirmary!"

Julian gave Gabriel a dismissive facial expression. "I have one thing I need to do first. I will go shortly."

"Do you swear? I promised Argolan that I would look after you for a couple of weeks."

"I swear. Just let me take care of one thing, and I'll meet you at the infirmary in fifteen minutes."

And off Gabriel went. Julian continued slowly down to his quarters. His physical condition had improved a little, but he was still very weak and in considerable pain. The only reason he was at all mobile at this point was that he had not been tortured for many weeks now.

Julian struggled all the way to his quarters. When he went inside the modest room, the lights were completely off for the first time in his memory. He told the computer to turn on the lights. It complied by turning on the very low-level lighting to which it had been programmed.

Julian went to the head of his bed and sat. He looked at the headboard where he kept his pictures and grabbed one of them.

Julian Paul had looked at the picture many times over the years but had never taken conscious note of this one detail. He held in his hands the picture of him and his parents on Etty Prime, which was taken when he was five years old. In the background, sitting on an observation table was the chest which the Focus had found in its recent exploits, or at least a chest that looked identical to it. How in the world had he come into contact with it twice? The odds must have been in the trillions to one.

Julian tucked the picture into his left pants pocket and headed very slowly down to the infirmary.

Chapter 44

The Fleet

Finally, after traveling at light speed for almost four weeks to the appointed rendezvous location, Argolan, from the bridge of the flagship, could see his fleet lying in wait, or at least what remained of his fleet.

"Scott, please send out a message to the Apex to signal our approach."

"Yes, Argolan," Scott Kilton, the flagship's communications director, replied to Argolan.

Naziz Kumar appeared on the viewer. "I am so thankful to see you again, and for that matter, your whole fleet. Were there any casualties, and is Julian with you?"

"No casualties, and Julian is okay. He will need some medical treatment, but all three of the med techs we brought to Eden confirmed that he will recover fully in due time," Argolan answered, while an obvious look of relief came over Kumar's face. "What is the status of the fleet?"

"It's small. We're down to five hundred sixty-one ships, and we're low on fuel and food. I have taken control of the fleet as the Grand Admiral, which of course, I relinquish to you now that you're back. However, there is a plus. The ships that made it out, by and large, were our most heavily armored and armed. If we are going to wage war, we are as well off as we could hope."

Argolan sneered. "Well, get ready for it. You can be sure that the Fifth Fleet is following. I want you to have the fleet ready to head to the Sigma System right away. I think we have made an ally there, and in this Galaxy with so many enemies near to us, it would be good to have a friend close by. Argolan out."

The screen shut off. In reality, Argolan would have preferred to move the fleet out right now, but that wasn't possible. To prepare a fleet of ships this large to move was a monumental undertaking if it was to be done without collisions.

"Scott, please raise the Liahona."

Eric Lopez, the Liahona's communications director, appeared on screen.

"Hi Argolan. Sir, it's good to have the fleet back together again, isn't it?"

"It really is," Argolan responded reflectively. "Would you please put me through to Julian or Gabriel?"

"Sure. They're in the infirmary. Transferring you now."

Doctor Marion Jensen appeared on the screen. He was a tall, thin man who looked exactly like a doctor. He was the director of medicine for the Empire and worked most of the time on board the Liahona, which had the most sophisticated medical lab in the Empire.

"Marion, how is Julian?"

"Argolan, he is literally doing better than he should be. I cannot account for it, but he is. I think he'll be at close to one hundred percent in just a few more days."

"That's great news! May I speak with him?"

"He's resting now, but as soon as he wakes up, I'll have him contact you."

"Thanks. Argolan out."

The screen went black.

Chapter 45

The Pursuit

Masse sat back in his command chair on the bridge of the Arcalis, the command ship of the Fifth Fleet. To his surprise, the Trade Empire's surprisingly small fleet did not head back to Sharanda but instead to the Sigma System. Clearly Argolan was now in league with that worm Williams. He would deal with Williams later.

The fleet kept a good distance. They monitored the Imperial Fleet over radar. Masse knew that the latest radar technology of the military, which was radically advanced, had a much greater range than the Trade Empire's radar technology, enabling the Fifth Fleet to monitor all that Argolan's fleet did without Argolan's fleet being able to see its pursuers.

This radar technology was enabled by what the military had come to call nanorelays. These were small robots that were made up of two components: A miniature light drive engine; and a radar amplifier. When a group of nanorelays was released, they positioned themselves between the listening party and the party being tracked. They were smaller than a pencil tip, and thereby were undetectable at these distances. They sent out the ping looking for their prey and relayed information back to the pursuer. This conceptually simple device had been a major advancement in technology, due to the engineering required to develop the small light-drive engines. Also, the logic programming which enabled the miniature robots to react to constantly changing circumstances had taken years of research and development.

"Mr. Nole, what is the Imperial fleet's destination?" Masse asked his executive officer.

"Sir, it appears to be Sigma Twelve, Sir."

"Put a stellar map depicting the Sigma System on my monitor. I want it to show the current position and orbits of all the planets in the system for the next seventy-two hours. I also want these coordinates, XMP12RJS, highlighted on Sigma Twelve."

The monitor next to Masse's command chair came to life. Of course he knew that all the planets in the Sigma System revolved around their sun in the same orbit at the same pace. He believed that if he watched the orbits take place on his monitor for long enough, with Williams's base of operations highlighted on Sigma Twelve, he would discover a set of circumstances which would leave Argolan blind to the Fifth Fleet's approach.

He did.

Chapter 46

A Plea for Help

The Trade Empire's fleet of more than five hundred fifty ships had barely entered the Sigma System when Kasis Williams appeared on the flagship bridge's viewer.

"I expect that we owe you a thank you," Argolan said to Williams with a hint of humorous sarcasm. "I suspect that you sent us to Masse with a guardian angel."

Argolan saw the vial which had once been on the neck of Zahn hanging around Williams's neck.

"I just gave you accurate information instead of the drivel Masse wanted me to pawn off on you. The rest…was up to you. I am glad that you were able to retrieve your son."

"How did he know these things?" Gabriel wondered, watching the conversation between the two men from the bridge of the Liahona. He was once again in awe of his uncle's knowledge of events.

Kasis and Argolan had formed an instant rapport in their first meeting. It made Gabriel uneasy. In fact, it made his skin crawl. Argolan had been like a surrogate father to him ever since his real father died. His parents had fled for their lives from this man and his organization, and now Argolan was becoming friendly with him.

"We're going to need some supplies. Food, fuel and some parts. Would you help?"

Kasis gazed on the image of Argolan. He could not believe it, but he was actually considering helping this man. In truth, Argolan had been one of his heroes from the time he was a young man. If there was one businessman in the Galaxy to emulate, it was he.

Argolan was warm, caring and also what Kasis most wanted to be but never could--honest. There was such a quality of genuineness to him that Kasis had never seen anything like it.

Kasis knew that when he had sent Argolan to bring Zahn to him, his code or whatever it was he lived by, would never allow him to do it. That was why Kasis had followed Argolan to Zahn. Kasis knew that Argolan hadn't been dishonest with him; Kasis had simply put him in an impossible position.

"All right!" Williams was stunned by his own answer. "We'll meet at our previous meeting place in thirty-two hours. I have business that I will be occupied with until then. Williams out."

"Scott, please put me through to Julian the in Liahona's infirmary," Argolan requested.

Kilton responded affirmatively, and a moment later Julian appeared on the screen.

"Finally, we may speak," Argolan said to him, absolutely beaming. He had thought at one point in time all of those months back that he would never have the chance to speak to this wonderful young man again.

"Father, thank you," was all that Julian said.

"I don't want to hold you up. You need to rest. I just wanted to tell you that I love you, and I'm sorry that you wound up in the center of my conflict. This should never have involved you."

"You have no need to apologize. I know you would have traded places with me if you could have," Julian replied with complete sincerity.

"Indeed. I knew you were strong. I knew that you would learn that for yourself eventually. Your purpose lies before you like a path. Walk that path. You, my son, will usher the Empire into its next era of greatness."

There was silence for a few moments. Argolan wanted to give Julian time to absorb his words and Julian attempted to do so. However, Julian was somewhat distracted.

"Father, I remembered where I have seen that chest before. I have a-"

Julian never had a chance to finish his sentence.

Chapter 47

Battle at Sigma

Julian began to hear loud thumping sounds, when, without warning, his link to the flagship was severed. He went to the porthole of the infirmary to investigate and saw a sight which few had ever seen.

Julian watched as an epic battle began to erupt. Apparently the Fifth Fleet had snuck up on the Empire's fleet. Perplexed, Julian wondered, "How do sixteen hundred interstellar warships sneak up on anyone?"

At first, the battle only involved the ATS Gridlock, which returned fire with its port gun turrets. Then the Foundation, the Suppression and the Focus joined in.

Gun-turret technology had come a long way in the past couple of decades. It used to take a few moments for the pulse emitter to cool after the turret fired, but no longer. Due to new cooling technologies, the emitter cooled so quickly, a single gun turret was now capable of firing three shots per second. Each of the Trade Empire's ships, having been armed to prepare for the inevitable conflict with the Guild, had twenty port and twenty starboard batteries. As a result each of these ships was lighting up space with between thirty-six-hundred and seventy-two-hundred rounds per minute, depending on which batteries were firing. And space was lit up. Dozens of ships were now involved in the battle with Sigma Twelve as the backdrop.

The Liahona lurched forward to come to bear on the Fifth Fleet. Julian recognized this as his cue to get to the bridge. He was no longer in medical scrubs, but in his civilian clothes, for he was due to be discharged today.

As Julian sprinted through the infirmary door he could hear Doctor Jensen yelling after him to stay, but he ignored the man's pleas. The trip up to the bridge was challenging because the Liahona had taken several direct hits, each hit jarring the entire behemoth.

When Julian finally arrived at the bridge Gabriel was giving instructions in his usual brilliant fashion. Julian was always in awe of the speed with which Gabriel could read a situation, analyze the best course of action to take and issue orders to arrive at his desired results. Julian made a mental note that understanding this skill of Gabriel's and learning how to teach it en masse would be an invaluable tool to the Empire in the future.

Gabriel saw Julian, rose from the command chair, went to a work station and updated his old friend, "Julian, we have an open stream with Naziz Kumar. He is running tactical," Gabriel updated Julian.

"How are we doing?" Julian asked.

"Pretty well, considering, but we're so massively outnumbered. It is going to take a miracle to save us."

"Naziz, give me my orders, please. The Liahona is at your disposal."

While Kumar gave the Liahona its instructions Julian watched the battle which raged on outside. He watched as the Nemesis sustained a series of explosions first at the stern of the ship, followed by a compartment blow-up in the mid-section. Next there was an explosion near the bow, then the nose of the ship blew. Suddenly the Nemesis was completely engulfed in flames. It began falling toward Sigma Twelve. As smaller secondary explosions occurred, pieces of shrapnel were ejected from the explosion. Occasionally one would go in the direction of the Liahona, and the scraping of metal could be heard against its shields.

The battle raged on for a couple of hours when Masse's signal came through to the Imperial flagship. In that time the Empire had taken massive losses, and, even though many of the Fifth Fleet's ships had been damaged or destroyed, the fleet had barely been scathed.

"Put him on general channels please, Scott," Argolan requested.

The bridge crew looked at Argolan, comprehending the order's significance.

Scott Kilton, the flagship's communications director, did so, and the madman, Masse, appeared on all the viewers on all the ships in both fleets. This was maritime tradition. When calling for terms of surrender, the signal was sent out fleet-wide to both sides of the conflict, so all hands understood the terms of surrender. Many cease fires had been interrupted when a zealous party who didn't understand the terms of the cease fire felt threatened and broke the truce.

The Madman smiled.

"So, Argolan, we have finally arrived at the apogee of our relationship."

"Do you mean to spare us?" Argolan asked, antagonistically.

"You, no. Your fleet, well, that depends on you. You have lost. Your fleet numbers less than two hundred now, and while you have done considerable damage to my fleet, our numbers are far too many for you."

"Name your terms." Normally Argolan would not have even entertained his terms, but this situation was different. The Empire's fleet *was lost*, and there was no point in sentencing his loyal friends to death today. Besides, perhaps a chance to get to Masse and end this conflict once and for all would present itself.

"First, I want the Soulseeker back. Second, I want you. I intend to pull you to pieces, to torture you, perhaps for many years to come. If you meet these terms, your fleet will go free with the caveat that I never see it again, not one ship from that pathetic assemblage."

"Masse, what assurance do I have?"

"What.. what as.. what assurance do you have? You arrogant, insignificant little....What choice do you have? If it weren't for that fact that I must have the Soulseeker, back I would destroy your entire fleet now! You have ten minutes to decide!" The screen went black.

"Scott, please open an encrypted thread to the bridge of the Liahona." Argolan knew that Julian, the man he had become, would have recognized when the battle began, that his place was on his bridge. The old Julian would have allowed his doctor to dictate his actions, forcing him to rest before returning to his duties. But no longer.

As Julian's grave face filled the monitor only one word came across, "Surrender?"

Argolan gave Julian a weak grin. "Not exactly. I am going to end this once and for all."

Julian's blood ran cold.

"Eric," Julian addressed Eric Lopez, the Liahona's director of communications, "please put this thread through to the station in my briefing chamber." Within five seconds Julian was in his private briefing chamber where Argolan's image was on the computer monitor, awaiting him.

"Father, what are you planning to do?"

"Far too many people have already paid the price for this personal dispute between James and me. It ends here. You are going to bring me the Soulseeker. I am going to load an anti-matter bomb on board her, land her on Masse's ship and blow it into tomorrow."

"You can't possibly believe that Masse is going to keep his word and let our fleet go!"

"Of course not. Once I have landed I will let him know that I have the bomb on board. I will then blackmail him into letting the fleet go. After all of our ships have left, I will detonate the bomb."

Julian's eyes welled up. "Father… you…you can't. I won't allow it. I need you. The Trade Empire needs you. I don't want to go on without you. I won't."

"Son, you have become a great man. You recently went to an extreme that most people would never have even considered to defend your beliefs. However, I am YOUR father. While I respect your opinion, you do not have dominion over me. This is the course we are going to take, and you will do your part in it." Argolan let the last statement hang.

"Yes, father," Julian said while closing the communications thread. Julian went down to the Soulseeker.

Argolan turned back to Kilton, "Please signal Admiral Masse."

The Madman's gloating face filled the bridge of Argolan's flagship. "The Soulseeker will be delivered to me within twenty minutes. It will take me about ten more minutes to pilot from my ship to yours. Then you will have me. Argolan out," he said cutting Masse off at the beginning of a sentence.

Chapter 48

The Sacrifice

Argolan stood in the landing bay of his ship watching the Soulseeker enter the hangar and put down. He turned to Young, who had come over to the flagship from the Focus with Abraham Kalman a short time earlier. "Lawrence, the fleet is yours. I am counting on you to support Julian as he runs the Empire. He is wise and intelligent but you have the real world experience he will need, understood?" Young only nodded, not making eye contact with Argolan.

"Don't be sad. We have had an extraordinary run together. That reminds me, I can never adequately express my gratitude for the loyalty you have shown to me over the years. You are the best friend that a man could have had, and you are a large part of the reason for the success of the Empire. I promise you that Julian will reward you appropriately. I am going to miss you." Argolan reached forward to embrace Young.

Young, who was a man of few words, returned the embrace and replied, "I will miss you too, my friend."

Julian disembarked and approached Argolan and Young. Julian gave Young a pleading look. "Lawrence, would you please give us some time alone?"

"Certainly," Young said. It wasn't the verbal response that surprised both Julian and Argolan, but that Young smiled at Julian. It was a sad smile but a smile nonetheless.

Young left.

"Father, there is no need for you to do this. It's frivolous suicide."

"That is not at all accurate." Argolan paused for a few moments. "Can you come up with any scenario in which we will win this battle?" Julian hesitated, hoping that Argolan would continue, but he didn't. Finally Julian became so uncomfortable with the silence that he answered.

"No."

"Tens of thousands of our people, people over whom I have responsibility, are still alive. We have more than two hundred ships still intact. The Empire can go on to see another day, the Empire under your leadership. Besides, too many people have been hurt as collateral damage in this private war between James Masse and me."

"Oh, so that's it. You feel guilty over Masse taking and torturing me!"

"How could I not? Julian, you mean more to me than you could ever imagine. You will never know the love that a father has for his children until you have a child of your own. It was my fault. I did not adequately prepare the Empire for Masse's imminent onslaught. That was my error, and it cost you dearly."

"I am fine. In fact, I went through some personal growth as a direct result of that experience. I rediscovered my faith in the Lord through my personal trial. I now understand that all things happen according to His will. I don't know if I ever would have been able to recover the faith of my childhood had things not transpired the way they did. You do not need to pay restitution, and even if you did, your suicide would not be restitution. If you want to repay me, stay alive!"

"Do you think that I want to die? I haven't seen your sister in years. The Empire is in one of the most crucial periods it has ever been. The economic and political structure of the Galaxy hangs in the balance. I want to see this next era ushered in, but not at the expense of our people."

Abraham Kalman and two of the flagship's scientists entered the landing bay wheeling a metal crate before them.

Argolan noticed the trio and called out to them, "Abraham, please have your men put that into the hold on the Soulseeker. While they are taking care of that, would you please come over here?"

The men complied.

When Kalman reached Julian and Argolan, he extended his hand toward Argolan. "Working with you has been one of the greatest experiences in my life."

That was saying a lot as Kalman had served for years on the Galactic Frontier exploring previously uncharted regions of space.

"For me too," Argolan replied returning the clasp. "Abraham, you have one of the most amazing minds that I have ever seen. Be well."

To Argolan's surprise Abraham remained, and Julian did not protest.

"Julian, just remember that I love you, and I know that you were put here for a great purpose. Strive every day to fulfill that purpose."

The two men embraced.

Chapter 49

Stowaway

Midway up the Soulseeker's boarding ramp Argolan stopped and turned to take one last look at his son. Interestingly, Julian wasn't paying any attention to him but instead was speaking with Kalman. Argolan shrugged, stepping up into the hold. He stopped at the metal case and scanned his thumb with the DNA reader on the case. It unlocked.

Argolan opened the lid to reveal the device. The bomb had an effective yield of approximately five teratons. It was actually strong enough to alter the orbit of a small planet. Fortunately an anti-matter bomb had never been used in waging war. A weapon like this was a planet killer. For all of man's imperfections, he had never engaged in genocide on a planetary scale. Argolan removed the trigger from the bomb and ran a few tests to make sure it was operational. These triggers had a tendency to malfunction, and he wanted to make certain that his sacrifice was not going to be in vain.

Argolan confirmed the trigger was functional, replaced it, relocked the case and went to the cockpit of the shuttle. Upon reaching the cockpit, with the push of a button, Argolan retracted the loading ramp and closed the hatch. He then engaged the anti-gravity thrusters and took off.

Argolan had about ten minutes until he would be delivering his "package" to the Madman, and he decided to use that time to pray. He thanked the Lord for the many blessings he had received in his life and asked for favor to be poured upon those for whom he cared. He had listed more than thirty people by name when he heard a sound from the hold of the small shuttle. He heard footsteps approaching, and the door to the cockpit opened.

Julian stepped into the small cockpit.

"Hey, dad!"

Julian never called Argolan "dad" except in play. This was one of two playful quips Julian used in reference to Argolan. However, this was not play time.

"Julian, what in the world?!" Argolan was actually angry.

"Hear me out---" Julian started, placing his hands up in a submissive posture.

"I can't believe you. After all the Empire risked saving you, after all that our friends risked for you, you pull something as senseless as this!" Argolan boomed at Julian.

"Father, please listen to me. Masse will never let the fleet continue. I spent enough time with him to know that he plans to erase all evidence of your existence, including me and Faith. In addition I have a plan. I think we can take out Masse's ship, disorient his fleet and escape with our lives and our ships."

Argolan was still angry with Julian, but he let it go. If they were to die he didn't want their last few moments together to be spent in anger. "Tell me your plan."

"When I was in the infirmary I read the reports that your team filed about the process of my rescue. One had spoken of a laser sweep which was set by Zahn against your team, but your team had anticipated it, found it, disarmed it and removed it. Being extraordinarily bored during my recovery I learned more about that technology because I could see many military applications. We may want to use that technology going forward. I tracked the laser sweep to your ship's science team."

"Of course," Argolan interjected, "They were the team that disarmed it on Sigma One."

"Before I went over to your ship, I contacted Abraham Kalman. I had him locate a Zorantham box."

A Zorantham box was a miniature facsimile of a Zorantham compartment. A Zorantham compartment, named after Georges Zorantham, was designed to jettison its contents should they become a threat while in space. Georges Zorantham and his crew fought in the battle of Osis Oni. In the course of the battle their anti-gravity pulse generator was damaged. Back then antigravity pulse generators were built into a ship as a permanent part. The damage to it had caused a breach in the outer shielding of the generator which continued to manufacture its pulse. The anti-gravity-pulses literally tore Zorantham's crew limb from limb. It was later determined that the breach had been gradual. It had started as a pinhole, not dangerous to anyone. However, each pulse ripped away a bigger and bigger chunk of the generator's shielding, eventually causing a full breach. If at any time during that lengthy process the generator could have been jettisoned, the crew would have probably survived.

The military's top engineers had gone to work to design a dump system for damaged anti-gravity pulse generators. What they developed was a compartment which would encapsulate the generator. This compartment was on a track, giving the engineering team the ability to jettison the compartment with the generator were it to become damaged. They aptly named the compartment after their beloved fallen comrade. A Zorantham box was a small, portable facsimile of a Zorantham compartment.

"While you were running through your pre-launch routines before takeoff, we welded the Zorantham box onto the exterior of the Soulseeker and placed the laser sweep in it. Once we have landed on Masse's ship, and the welcoming party has arrived to meet us, I intent to jettison the sweep and activate it remotely. That will clear the landing bay of everyone. Next we'll unload the bomb, take off and detonate it remotely. It may not work, but I am not going to allow you to die without a fight."

"This is about the most ridiculous plan I have ever heard. We are both going to die now."

"Have faith, father."

Although Argolan would never have admitted it to Julian because he felt that Julian had let his emotions eclipse his judgment, he was very proud of him at this moment. Putting himself in harm's way like this was something that Julian never could have done ten months earlier. Nor would he ever have taken charge of the situation this way. He had truly grown.

"All right, we'll do it your way but you are to stay out of harm's way. Got that?"

"Yes, sir," Julian responded with his other playful quip.

Chapter 50

The Monster

As Masse watched the Soulseeker land on the bridge's monitor he was salivating. All of his work, all of these years, and here, finally, his prize lay right before him. However, if Masse had learned anything about Argolan over these past few months, it was not to underestimate him. Just a few days earlier he had had Argolan in a very similar situation where he had voluntarily walked straight into a trap, and Masse had grown overconfident. As a result, Argolan still breathed today. But not this time. This time Masse wasn't leaving anything to chance. He had sent the ship's entire complement of soldiers to the landing bay to meet Argolan.

The ship's landing seemed to take forever. Once again Masse felt like a child on Christmas Eve. First, the ship entered the landing bay. Next, the landing braces extended. Then finally, the ship put down. But the hatch didn't open.

Masse felt the Monster rising within him. In fact, he felt it begin to overtake him. He had been fighting this for a long time, but he had really known for the past several years that at some point, he would no longer have any control over the Monster, that he would not be able to push it back into the shadows.

Masse yelled frantically into the intercom to his men. "Report!!"

He could see on his monitor that his men in the landing bay were somewhat unsure of what to do.

"He's not disembarking, sir."

Masse watched as his men approached the shuttle.

"Then have your welder start to work on opening the hatch!" Masse shouted. On the monitor he could see his men shrink as he raised his full, strong voice. He observed the team's welder come through the numerous rows of heavily armed SEALs, who completely engulfed the shuttle and get to the front of the throngs to begin work on the hatch.

Just then Masse saw what he thought was perhaps his imagination playing a trick on him. It appeared as if something leapt from the side of the shuttle and landed on the floor in the middle of the crowd. He quickly realized, however, that it wasn't his imagination, as it had caught the attention of some of his men as well.

Frantically Masse screamed into the intercom, "Get out of there! It's a trap."

But it was too late. He watched as every man in the landing bay was sliced into slivers by a laser sweep. Worse yet, he recognized it by its dispersal pattern as being one of his own, one that he had traded to Zahn in a prior business transaction.

The rest of Masse's bridge crew gasped. They had all just lost long-time colleagues and friends in the most gruesome of deaths imaginable.

The Monster came unleashed. The small remnant of Masse which had remained for the past thirty-six years was now fully consumed by the Monster, and it was pure evil.

Masse stood up from his command chair and removed his sidearm. As Masse made his way to the exit to leave the bridge, two of his officers stepped in front of him.

"Sir," Petty Officer First Class Jones said, "I think you should stay here for your own safety."

The Monster had no regard for human life. All it wanted was to quench its lust for revenge. It lifted its sidearm and quickly fired laser bolts into both men.

The two remaining bridge officers moved quickly, but the Monster was faster. Before the two men could stand up from the work stations at which they sat, they had cauterized holes in their chests, and their corpses fell onto their consoles. The Monster left the bridge of its ship for the last time and ran full-speed for the landing bay.

Chapter 51

The Monster and the Hero

The bomb was now out of the Soulseeker's hold. Julian and Argolan pushed the wheeled case through the field of human remains and away from the shuttle to give it clearance room for take off. Julian, who had been listening carefully, heard someone approaching. He immediately stopped, signaled to Argolan to hide and ran behind a stack of crates to the side of the door leading out of the landing bay. The crates would keep him hidden from anyone entering the room.

Argolan tripped over a body part and fell. He got up, but it was too late. The door opened, and the Serpent didn't delay. He fired three rounds toward Argolan. The first two missed, but the third caught Argolan in the left shoulder, spun him around and threw him to the floor. Masse was an expert marksman. He seldom missed his mark. The only reason he hadn't hit Argolan square in the chest was because he had been running while he fired his sidearm. Still his shot had been true enough to hit its mark.

As the Serpent ran to the edge of the crates which were in front of the door, the hidden Julian hit him in the throat with his right elbow. This doubled the Serpent over as he grabbed his throat and coughed. Julian leapt toward the Serpent and grabbed the gun by the barrel with both of his hands. The Serpent was astoundingly strong for man his age. He pushed back, grabbing the grip of the pistol with both hands.

The Serpent was actually strong enough that he was able to twirl Julian around and then push him backward, slamming him into the bulkhead behind him.

The Serpent was too strong. As hard as Julian resisted, the Serpent slowly moved the gun's barrel from the left of Julian's head closer and closer to his temple. Julian couldn't resist anymore; he pulled the gun toward and passed himself using the Serpent's own momentum to pass the gun quickly over his body. The Serpent pulled the trigger, and the shot missed Julian's head hitting the bulkhead just above his right shoulder.

The gun was now to the right of Julian's head, and he struggled to keep it there, and once again he was overwhelmed. The gun moved closer and closer to being pointed directly at Julian's head, and again Julian used the Serpent's own balance to move the barrel quickly past his head. Now the Serpent shot the bulkhead just over Julian's left shoulder. This time, however, Julian had used enough force to have the Serpent's gun go well past his body, throwing the Serpent off balance.

When the Serpent stumbled, Julian removed his right hand from the barrel of the gun, reached down to the Serpent's utility belt and removed the gun that he had used to plant the charges in the walls of Mount Efil for his escape. As Julian did so, the Serpent's belt unclasped and fell to the floor. Julian put the barrel of the gun up against the left side of the Serpent's neck and pulled the trigger. There was a thud. The Serpent suddenly stood straight up, put his left hand over the puncture wound and dropped his sidearm. Blood oozed between his fingers.

Julian bent down and grabbed the belt. He stepped back and pushed the red button on the belt. The charged separated Masse's head from his torso; both fell to the floor.

Julian sprinted over to Argolan who was conscious but still on the floor.

"Father!" Julian exclaimed as he ran over to Argolan to help him rise.

"I'm fine. Those military sidearms have considerable concussion when they land a shot. Let's get out of here."

"Yeah," was all Julian could manage, not really being able to believe what had just transpired. He had just been responsible for hundreds of human deaths. He knew that he had had no option, yet the thought made him ill. And the worst part was that he hadn't finished yet.

Chapter 52

Last Embrace

"Julian, how far are we from the Arcalis?"

Julian worked on the navigation computer.

"We're sixty seven-thousand kilometers away from it, little over halfway back to the Imperial Fleet."

"Good," Argolan sighed.

The Soulseeker had been picked up on radar by the other ships of the Fifth Fleet from the moment of lift off. Hail after hail had come in which the Soulseeker hadn't answered. No commander in his right mind would have fired on the Soulseeker without express permission. Now it was time to put on a show for those commanders.

Argolan punched a sequence of numbers on the computer terminal in the Soulseeker's cockpit, and a sickening sound blasted from outside the shuttle. Julian watched out of the aft porthole as the monumental explosion occurred. It was the size of a small planet, sending shrapnel everywhere. Julian could hear the clinking of shrapnel hitting the shuttle's shields.

Unfortunately, there was such a massive residual energy well in the immediate area that communications signals couldn't get through.

"Father, do you have any idea how long it will be until we can communicate with the fleet?"

"Not exactly, but I suspect that we will be able to have you back on your ship before that occurs."

A few minutes later they were back on the Liahona running to the bridge. The bridge crew was ecstatic to see them alive again, but Julian quickly squelched any celebratory gestures.

"Gabriel, what's the fleet's status?"

"There is a massive wall of debris now separating the two fleets. My scans are spotty at best but, the Fifth Fleet appears to be massing in an attempt to go around it."

"Do you have an ETA?"

"At least fifteen more minutes."

"How quickly can we have our fleet positioned to get out of here?"

Gabriel looked at radar readings, ran a short mental analysis and answered, "It looks like we will be ready in about ten minutes."

"How will we be able to do it so soon?" asked Julian.

"We have been planning for the jump since just after you left the Liahona on the Soulseeker."

Julian smiled at Argolan.

"You didn't *really* think that I believed he would let the fleet go, did you?" Argolan chided Julian.

Every minute that Julian spent with Argolan, Argolan amazed him more and more.

"I am going back to the flagship. I can be there in five minutes. That will leave plenty of time. It's going to be tricky to coordinate our escape without communications." Then, as if was an afterthought, Argolan added, "Thank you for saving my life!"

Although he didn't think it was a good idea for Argolan to return to his ship in the midst of all that was happening, Julian was not going to question him anymore after this day. Julian stepped forward, gave him a hug and said, "I love you, and I want you to know that I would do anything, even die, for you."

"I know."

Argolan left. Julian redirected his attention to Gabriel.

"What is the last communication we had with Naziz Kumar?"

While Gabriel was giving Julian the tactical update, they saw a laser volley launched signaling that Argolan was safely back onboard the flagship.

Chapter 53

Intervening Force

Julian paused and looked at the debris field. In his mind's eye he visualized how he believed the Fifth Fleet was going to move using the bits and pieces of what he could see through the field as a guide, while simultaneously visualizing and how the field was dissipating. He then interlaced the two separate images in his mind. This technique, which Julian called, "Three Dimensional Interlacing," was a technique he had developed as a result of studying Gabriel's analytical abilities. Unfortunately radar was still barely functioning due to the residual energy. Even Gabriel, who was a master of this technique, with his lightning-fast mind, couldn't gather enough data to perform a well-founded analysis.

"I don't think we're going to make it Gabriel." Julian said in a slightly panicked tone of voice.

"I don't know, Julian. I can't gather enough data to analyze. Preparing the fleet for a jump to light speed without verbal communication is proving more difficult than anticipated. However, the good news is that the communications outage is certainly affecting the Fifth Fleet's ability to coordinate movement as well," Gabriel reported.

"No, my friend," Julian took the opportunity to teach Gabriel, "The Fifth Fleet trains extensively for contingencies just like this. They are paralyzed and off balance because of the loss of the command ship but will soon regain their equilibrium. We must move quickly, or all of our efforts here today will be lost."

Finally the remaining debris and energy fields were beginning to dissipate, revealing the Fifth Fleet's position to the Empire's fleet. Of course the opposite was true as well. When revealed, the Fifth Fleet was in the exact position Julian had anticipated.

Unfortunately, coordinated navigation for light jump without voice communications being open was never a contingency for which the Empire's fleet had trained. Luckily communications were starting to return intermittently.

"Julian, we have a wide spectrum inter-ship communications link coming over comm," Eric Lopez, a newer addition to the Liahona's bridge staff reported.

"Accept, and put through please."

A wide spectrum communications link was a highly encrypted audio-only link. It enabled many ships to communicate or participate in the same conversation at the same time while not being slowed down much due to the encryption. It was typically used during battles to send real-time messages throughout a fleet. Encrypted video links always had longer lag times.

The complete leadership of the fleet was present on this call.

"All," Argolan began, "We have Commander Young and Naziz Kumar on channel with us. Naziz, please give us some tactical direction here."

Once again, Argolan displayed his humility and wisdom in surrounding himself with people to whose expertise he would submit.

Naziz weighed in. "All, please put your viewers onto the debris field. The Fifth Fleet is reorganizing. It has started to move its armada to circumnavigate the field. We are not going to be able to jump before their fleet has a clear line of fire on us. Also, we can not jump from here. Now that the energy levels have waned, and we have new radar readings of the area, we can see that there is much too much local debris for a clean jump. Thank goodness that we didn't attempt this earlier. It could have proven disastrous."

It was standard protocol to scan the immediate area before a jump to light speed. Moving that quickly even a small piece of debris could penetrate shielding and put a hole in the hull of a ship.

Naziz continued. "I recommend that we move with full thrusters one-hundred-eighty degrees away from the debris field while the Fifth Fleet loses time going around. When we hit the Johnson Slipstream we will make our jump to the pre-assigned coordinates"

"All in agreement?" Argolan polled.

"Yea."

"Yea."

"I concur, too," Argolan inserted. "Let's move the fleet out now. Leave this channel open but muted for real-time tactical communications from Naziz."

A message went out to the fleet. To move a fleet at full thruster speeds took little to no coordination because one could navigate manually. There was time to make heading adjustments. With a light jump there wasn't.

"Okay, Drew, take us away from the debris field, thrusters at full."

"Okay" Drew Giles responded. He had been the Liahona's navigations lead for years, and he was an expert. He had the most acutely developed ability to pilot manually that Julian had ever seen. At that moment it dawned on Julian that the Empire really was a collection of "the best of the best." Economic opportunity draws excellence to itself.

As the Liahona moved, slowly at first, then gradually picking up speed, away from the debris field, Julian watched two separate events taking place. He watched the monitor on the bulkhead of the bridge which was displaying the debris field. Through the debris the Fifth Fleet could be seen scrambling into position to come about on the Empire's fleet once again. At the same time Julian watched the Imperial fleet move to put some distance between itself and the debris field on the monitor which sat just to the right of his command chair.

He could see that they weren't going to make it. The prey just wasn't moving quickly enough to outrun the hunter. Julian took the communications channel off mute. He said, "Father."

Argolan responded with despair, "I know. I know."

Over the next seven or eight minutes, the Empire's fleet continued to flee, and unfortunately the enemy armada continued to come about. Once the Fifth Fleet had cleared the debris field, the battle erupted again. As each ship of the Fifth Fleet cleared, they opened fire. The trade Empire's fleet was diminishing quickly.

Suddenly, as if out of nowhere, a ship appeared directly between the two fleets. Both armadas, somewhat confused, ceased fire.

Kumar's voice screamed over the comm, "Argolan, that appears to be the ship that attacked Sharanda!"

All communications stopped. In fact, everything stopped. Seconds which seemed like minutes to Julian passed, as all were frozen.

Then a distinctly non-human voice was broadcast over the Imperial fleet's communications wave. It said something incomprehensible.

Julian stood and watched the bridge viewer anxiously as the alien ship hovered in the middle of what just moments before had been the largest battlefield in the history of human warfare. His pulse was racing.

Quiet.

Stillness.

The alien vessel fired some kind of energy weapon. The blast struck the ATS Julian. The ball of energy went through the shield and then right into the ship itself. There was a blinding flash, and the ship was destroyed.

Chapter 54

The Loss

Julian's jaw dropped, and his legs gave out. Nauseated, he fell back into his chair, which luckily was right behind him. The charred remains of what had been the flagship of the Trade Empire began to plummet toward Sigma Twelve. Tears rushed to Julian's eyes. His father. His friend. His mentor. Gone.

There had been another flagship, a predecessor to the Julian, the Faith. When the Faith was destroyed about twenty years ago, Argolan christened its replacement the ATS Julian.

Both fleets turned their weapons on this alien ship. It fired back. The alien vessel appeared to be taking no damage while any ship that was touched by its weapon was destroyed instantaneously.

The ever-pragmatic Naziz came over the comm. "We need to retreat now!"

Also horrified, but able to think, Gabriel looked over at Julian, who was still speechless.

"All right Naziz," Gabriel became a surrogate for Julian. "Follow the pre-planned course. Send a message out to the fleet to follow."

As the Empire's fleet fled, the viewer on the Liahona's bridge displayed the battle between the alien vessel and the Fifth Fleet. It was not going at all well for the Fleet.

The fleet had already put the battle far behind itself when Julian finally spoke, breaking the loud silence.

"Naziz, do we have an audio recording of that communication from the alien vessel?"

"Of course. All communications streams are recorded during battle; it's Imperial policy."

"Is the Linguistics Foundation ship still with the fleet?" Julian asked the newly appointed tactical director.

"Yes, why?"

"Get them a recording of the transmission, the original first officer's log which the Focus found and all of the files the Intelligence Center created while studying the alien log. I want to attempt to get a translation of the communication."

"Julian, I'll certainly comply, but wouldn't the Intelligence Center be the right ones for this job?"

Julian could no longer fight back the tears thinking back to the very similar conversation he had with his father back on Sharanda.

"No, not when we have a starting point. The Center 'cracked the code' when deciphering the log, and now with a place from which to start, this falls under the core competency of the Linguistics Foundation."

"A wise perception, Julian. I'll see to it. Kumar out." The stream was terminated.

"Not my wisdom," Julian thought, "Argolan's."

Chapter 55

Faith

Four days later the Liahona joined the fleet which had regrouped just outside of the Ranis System. Through a battle which had destroyed many ships, the Liahona had once again delivered her crew home safely.

The Ranis System was a dangerous star system due to the war between Ranis and Embuieck. This made it the perfect place in which to avoid detection because there was almost no traffic coming or going. The Empire's fleet needed a little down time and would most likely be relatively safe here as long as it could stay out of the struggle.

For the past few days, Julian had been trying fruitlessly to make contact with Faith to inform her of Argolan's death. She lived with her husband on a paradisiacal world named Herrin, located immediately on the other side of the Norson Expanse, where they ruled as king and queen. He had wanted to invite her to the memorial service which had just ended but had been unable to do so. It was not unusual for Faith to require time to return messages; her duties as queen of Herrin kept her very busy. This time, however, the long delay in response concerned Julian. He had tried to contact his brother-in-law, as well as the authorities on Herrin, but he had been stonewalled by secretaries and bureaucrats every step of the way.

Julian finally reached his quarters, still numb, due to recent events. He had lost so many friends in the past week he couldn't keep them straight. And of course there was the loss of Argolan. What was he going to do without him?

He entered and went to his bed. Julian lay on his back, looking up at the ceiling with his hands clasped behind his head, when there was a knock. He got up and opened the door. There stood Lawrence Young.

"Julian, may I speak to you for a moment?"

"Of course, come in," Julian replied stepping aside and politely waving Young into his quarters. Young had come on board the Liahona for the memorial service.

Young began by making small talk; it was not one of his strengths. "It was a very nice service." Julian neither replied nor looked at Young, not to be rude; he just didn't yet have the energy to get into it again with Young.

"I am sorry about your father," Young said very tenderly, something uncharacteristic of him. This did elicit a look and a response from Julian.

"Thank you, Lawrence. I know you loved him, too." Young had already offered his condolences at the memorial service. Julian wondered why Young didn't just come out and tell him why he was here. Young drew a deep breath which he slowly let out through his mouth. "This isn't easy for me to say, but I'm going to do my best." Young paused for a moment while collecting his thoughts.

He continued, "I know I have been…difficult toward you over the years, but I wanted to let you know that it's done. I finally comprehend. I understand the relationship the two of you shared. I understand the love that he had for you. Goodness, he's been telling me for years, but when I saw him at the moment we recovered you, I finally *understood*. I also see the strong leader you have become. I came to tell you that you don't have to worry about me blocking you anymore. You have my complete and total loyalty, as did your father."

With that Young turned to leave, but Julian said, "Lawrence, wait!" Young stopped and straightened up, but he didn't turn around. "That means a lot to me, and I know that it would to Argolan also. Thank you."

Young left.

Chapter 56

Another Secret Conversation

"Julian is going to take the remains of the Empire full military. Sharanda is the past. Its new seat of power is going to be Sigma Twelve," he said to the dark figure with piercing grey eyes on his monitor.

Grey Eyes reflected for a moment. "Is Paul going to be able to maintain the commerce infrastructure? That MUST stay intact."

"He thinks he will. He is kind of a visionary like his father was. I suspect he'll succeed."

"I will expect regular tactical updates from you regarding the militarization of the Empire."

"I can't do that," he replied to Grey Eyes. "I won't betray him or the Empire."

"You will give us the information we need. The Guild must be able to assume control of the New Territory's economy peacefully. You owe us; we helped you."

"I have given you so much information over the past two years that I would say we are more than even at this point."

The figure shifted.

"With that information you have already betrayed your friend and the Empire. The difference is if you don't provide me with what I want, I will have you exposed within the Empire. We have other eyes within its ranks that can arrange this. You no longer have the leverage to determine any of the parameters of our relationship. I went through a lot of trouble to put you in touch with Kasis Williams. You owe ME."

Now Gabriel shifted. What if he was exposed? What would he do? He didn't know how to respond.

"I will give you a couple of days to rethink your position." The Grey Eyes disappeared from his monitor.

Gabriel placed his elbows on his desk in the corner of his quarters, and dropped his head into his hands.

Chapter 57

Transmission Translated

While Julian worked at the desk in his briefing chamber just off the Liahona's bridge, he reflected on the events of the past year. It had now been almost a month since Argolan's death. It was curious how Julian's recent measurement of time always seemed to revolve solely around that event.

In the past month Julian had been quite busy trying to put his shattered Empire back together. He had assumed control of the Trade Empire with surprising ease. He didn't know if that was because Argolan had always set the expectation that Julian would succeed him in the minds of their employees or if it was because of Julian's newfound strength. Either way, true to his word, Young had been a tremendous help.

Simultaneously, Julian had been working to establish a new base of operations for the Trade Empire on Sigma Twelve. He was attempting to prepare the Trade Empire for the coming war with the Guild. He also, and this was the trickiest item on his agenda, was trying to reestablish the regional commerce infrastructure. If commerce atrophied in the region, worlds which currently were allies of the Empire because it served their economic purposes would begin to fall away. Julian could not afford to let this happen. These worlds needed to be made to see their vested interest in the continuing success of the Empire.

Julian paused from his work and looked at the picture of himself, Argolan and Faith which he kept on his desk. His prior concern over Faith's fate was evolving into acute trepidation. Multiple attempts to establish contact with Faith, her husband and their family had been stonewalled by various members of Herrin's ambassadorial establishment. Something was amiss there.

A chime interrupted Julian's thoughts. He sighed, pushed the chair in which he sat back from his desk, got up and opened the door to expose Ronald Tse. He was the courier on the Liahona.

"Julian, this just came for you from the Linguistics Foundation ship." Ronald handed Julian a Data Journal.

Julian took the Journal. "Thank you, Ron," he said. The door closed.

Julian placed his thumb in the DNA reader on the data journal and it came to life. He opened the first file titled "Cover Letter." It read:

Mr. Paul,
Contained in this classified journal you will find a translation of the message sent from the alien vessel. We were able to cross reference the deciphering of the alien's written language which was done by the Intelligence Center with the audio files of the transmission contained in the log and have come up with a working model for their verbal language. While the language contained in the message is not identical to the language contained in the journal they are clearly offshoots of the same base language. We believe our model to be 99.999 percent accurate. Thank you for providing the Foundation a chance to serve you.

Sincerely,
Amanda Ross
Managing Director
Linguistics Foundation
A division of the Argalian Trade Empire

Julian sat down on the chair at his desk, elbows on knees, with his hands which were holding the journal between his legs. He now opened the next file which was titled "Alien Message Translation v4972."

The file opened. Julian read it and a chill ran down his spine. The Data Journal dropped from Julian's hand and fell to the floor. He couldn't believe the text it contained. It simply read:

Argolan, you have betrayed us for the last time.

End Part 2

Appendix A
Glossary and Pronunciation Guide

Abraham Kalman-ATS Focus's director of science; generally considered to be one of the preeminent scientists within the Trade Federation

Aft-The back of a vessel

Amanda Ross-The Linguistics Foundation's managing Director

Angel-Argolan's wife (deceased)

Anti Gravity-Term pertaining to any number of devices employing a technology which repelled from gravity enabling objects move away from gravity's center

Arcalis (ahr-**kal**-uhs)-James Masse's command ship or flagship

Argalian (ahr-**gey**-lee-uhn) **Trade Empire**-A salvage and commerce organization named for and founded by Argolan; also referred to as the Empire or the Trade Empire

Argalian (ahr-**gey**-lee-uhn) **Trade Ship (ATS)**-Any bulk ship owned and operated by the Argalian Trade Empire

Argalian Hover-Skiff (AHS) Horizon-A skiff used to patrol the exterior of Mount Efil employing combustion engines in order to achieve air worthiness on Sharanda; this skiff was not a practical line of defense, but rather a means of attachment to Man's past via employment of a sentry

Argolan (ahr-**goh**-lin)-Founder of the Argalian Trade Empire; Husband to Angel (deceased); father to Faith and Julian Paul, his adoptive son

Armish (**ahrm**-ish) **Conklin**-Argolan's alias, created by Kasis Williams, used for a meeting with Zahn on Sigma One

ATS Focus-Ship commanded by Commander Lawrence Young; first ship after Argolan's original ship; named by Young after his self-perceived greatest asset

ATS Liahona (lee-yuh-**hoh**-nuh)-Ship commanded by Julian Paul; named after a device the Lord provided the ancients with to help them find His desired destination for them

Augustine-A white dwarf star located at one end of the Norson Expanse with the Blanner Black Hole at the other end

Azuri (az-**ur**-ee)**Canyon**-A very deep canyon located approximately 200 miles southwest of Mount Efil cut through a mountain range by the only above-surface river on Sharanda

Battery-A group of guns on a warship of the same caliber, used for the same purpose

Blanner Black Hole-A Black Hole located at one end of the Norson Expanse with Augustine at the other end

Blaster-Another turn for a laser gun

Brian Schultz-The ATS Focus's secondary or junior scientist

Bulkhead-Walls separating the interior of a ship into compartments

Captain--An honorary title sometimes given to upper-level management employees of the Trade Empire who managed ships; interchangeable with commander

Captain Donahue-See Donahue

Captain Split Jackson-See Split Jackson

Chan An'ur (chan uhn-**er**)-The key component of a weapon of unprecedented destructive power; while the Chan An'ur's origin was a well kept secret, the race that controlled it built this weapon to conquer the galaxy; the weapon was stolen and ultimately dismantled by an enemy race

Chemical Chisel-A process developed by a project team on the ATS Focus in which chemicals were introduced to an object in conjunction with a hypothermic laser to break the outer layer of the object away

Chief Petty Officer-The highest rank achievable to enlisted personnel in the Republic's Navy

Chris Connors-One of many security squad leaders for the Argalian Trade Empire

Command Ship-The ship from which the leader of a fleet disseminated orders; also referred to as flagship

Commander Lawrence Young-See Lawrence Young

Commander-An honorary title sometimes given to upper-level management employees of the Trade Empire who managed ships; interchangeable with captain

Computer Operator-A person within one of several departments in the Empire, computer operators specialized in using, repairing, hacking, and writing programs for computers

Controlled Area-A sterile room created by force field walls, ceiling, hallway and door intended to partition work areas for the safety of surrounding areas

Crime Syndicate-Any one of a group of organizations hailing from the Sigma System which engaged in elicit business activity on an interplanetary scale

Cryptography and Intelligence Center-One of the four divisions of the Argalian Trade Empire which primarily dealt with code-cracking

Dan Small-The ATS Focus's number one or primary computer operator

David Stein-ATS Focus's dock engineering team director

Dean Bennette-The ATS Liahona's director of security

Deck-The floor on a ship

Deirdre Lane-Director of communications for the Argalian Trade Empire

Democratic Republic-A form of government defined by two characteristics; a democracy (rule by majority) and a constitution (rule bylaw); the United States was founded as a democratic republic with the purpose that people would have a say in how the country was run, while at the same time guaranteeing the individual certain rights that even the majority couldn't override;

Department-A segment of one of the Argalian Trade Empire's divisions, some of which included: science and engineering, security, dock engineering, communications, medical, operations, operations, computers and project management; with some variations the Empire's hierarchy is broken into departments which are then duplicated in the fleet; reference Appendix B

Division-Any one of four separate sections comprising the Argalian Trade Empire including: Fleet, the Cryptography and Intelligence Center, the Linguistics Foundation and the Imperial Legal Alliance; each division was broken down into departments which segregated the division into working units; the number divisions within the Empire fluctuated due to needs; as needs arose new divisions ware delineated and as needs waned, certain divisions ware decommissioned; reference Appendix B

Dock Engineering Team Director-A highly specialized person at the head of the Dock Engineering team whose roll was to measure data pertaining to dock integrity to make sure that a breach of dock integrity did not occur

Donahue-Captain of the Arcalis, Donahue was a Republic Loyalist, who, while realizing that Masse did not have the best interests of the Republic at heart, did not oppose him due to fear that Masse would execute him

Drake Stetson-The Flagship's assistant manager

Drew Davies-The Flagship's director of security

Drew Giles-The ATS Liahona's navigations lead

Eden-A planet in the No'on system; home to James Masse's "secret" base; see No'on System

Embuieck (em-**byoo**-wek)- Planet located in the Ranis System; at war with neighboring planet Ranis

Eric Lopez-The ATS Liahona's Communications director

Etty (**et**-ee) **Prime**-A small world which once contained a mining colony until it was attacked by an alien armada; Etty Prime was never resettled; the world where Julian Paul was orphaned

Expansion Wars-The darkest era of Mankind's history when wars were fought over the rights to settle specific regions of the New Territories; two of the most famous battles in this war were the Battle of Osis Oni and the Battle of the No'on system

Faith-Daughter of Argolan; older sister of Julian Paul

Flagship-See command ship

Focus-See ATS Focus

Force Field-A wall of energy, usually created to form a partition; there are various types of force fields appropriate to different environments and tasks

Forward-The front of a vessel

Gabriel Williams-ATS Liahona's crew manager; best friend of Julian Paul

Galactic Democratic Republic (The Republic)-The governing body in the known Galaxy; this once great Republic, modeled after the government of the United States of America, fell to subversion of the constitution by the judges and lawyers of the Lawyers Guild, changing the it from a democratic republic into an oligarchy (rule by a select few)

Galafon (gal-uh-fon) **System**- The star system which is home to Sharanda and borders the Norson Expanse

Gayle Chase-The Argalian Trade Empire's director of operations; absent during most of this volume due to a special assignment given to her by Argolan

Georges (zawr-**an**-thuhm) **Zorantham**-A highly embellished war hero, captain of a ship whose crew met with a disaster due to a damaged anti-gravity pulse generator

Grey Eyes-A shadow enshrouded character with piercing grey eyes; presented self as a Republic loyalist to some and as a Guild loyalist to others

Haron (har-on) **System**-Not to be confused with the Herrin System, this system of three inhabited worlds bordered the Norson Expanse in the Old Territories; neighbor to the Opus System

Helmsman-The person who steered a ship

Herrin-A paradisiacal world bordering the Norson Expanse in the Old territories; ruled by King Benjamin and Queens Faith (Argolan's Daughter); the major tourist attraction in the galaxy, Herrin is known for its pleasantly dry, temperate atmosphere with lush rolling hills and white sand beaches

Horizon-See Argalian Hover Skiff Horizon

Hypothermic Laser/Hypothermic Beam-A laser which shots a very cold ray

Imperial Legal Alliance-A division of the Argalian Trade Empire chartered by Faith in order to meet the increasingly complex regulation of the trade industry, this division has three departments: licensing, which assures all procedures are properly licensed, accounting, which ensures all financial regulation is followed and interpretation, which studies the law on the book to ensure all legal protocols are followed and no laws are breached

James (Jim) Masse-The most highly decorated Naval officer in history and admiral over the renown Fifth Fleet; wanted revenge on Argolan for perceived past betrayal

Johnson Slipstream -An area in space, not far from the No'on system with a very strong, inexplicable current, which obscured radar, making it an ideal place to move a fleet undetected

Julian Paul-Lone survivor of the only attack on Man by an alien race, at Etty Prime mining colony, adoptive son of Argolan; brother of Faith

Kasis (key-sis**) Williams**-Identical twin brother of Gabriel Williams's father; head of the Oralti Crime Syndicate, Wife Dorothy

Lance Charles-Security Manager on the ATS Focus; directed security on the project team that encountered the alien derelict vessel

Laser Pistol-A handgun which shot a highly focused beam of light

Lawrence Young-Manager of the AST Focus; Commander Young was one of the first employees of the Trade Empire; although one of Argolan's closest friends, did not like Julian Paul

Lawyers Guild-A federation of lawyers bent on Galactic domination through subversive control of the Galactic Democratic Republic; this control was largely achieved by appointment of judges who undermined the constitution with their rulings; also referred to as The Guild

Liahona (lee-yuh-**hoh**-nuh)-A device given by the Lord to the ancients fleeing Jerusalem to direct them to the promise land; also see ATS Liahona

Light Engine-A system of laser emitters on the stern of a ship which fire at specific points on the back of the ship where a highly complex energy shield is located. The combination of the lasers and the shield created a physical interaction pushing the ship on the beams of light almost as two magnets with the same pole in line would repel each other

Linguistics Foundation-One of the four divisions of the Argalian Trade Empire which primarily assisted in communication with other humans and translation of their languages

Lyle Nole-James Masse's executive officer

Machinist-A position within the Empire, falling within the Science and Engineering department, which specialized in using precise machinery to work with metal and other substances to perform tasks such as creating specified parts for machinery

Marco Toms-Assistant director of operations for the Argalian Trade Empire

Marion (male) Jensen-Empire's director of medicine; works on the AST Liahona

Mickey Overton-ATS Focus's machinist

Mount Efil (e-**feel**)-A large mountain range located on Sharanda; contained an intra-mountain complex which housed the headquarters of the Argalian Trade Empire

Nancy Towne-Wife of Oliver Towne; mother of two young sons

Nanorelay-Miniature robots made up of a micro light drive engine and a radar amplifier; used by the Navy to extend radar reach

Naval Command-Command structure for the constitutionally created Navy; used to be loyal to the Republic but has been corrupted by the Guild

Naziz Kumar-The director of security for the Argalian Trade Empire; spent many years diligently studying military tactics in an attempt to prepare the Empire for war

New Territories-Settled region of space on Sharanda's side of the Norson Expanse; while the Galactic Democratic Republic technically had jurisdiction over the New Territories' the only regulatory arm of the Republic in the New Territories was the Sigma Commerce Bureau, which was far too small to enforce law in the region; as a result, the jurisdiction of the Republic in this region coupled with its the lack of presence, there was no unifying governing body there, instead this region was held together by interdependent commerce and trade

No'on (no-**on**) **System**-A remote start system which contained a world named Eden' James Masse's "secret" base of operations; unbeknownst to Masse Eden was not a secret but Naval Command and the Guild allowed Masse to operate under that illusion; other than Masse's base, No'on was uninhabited

Norson (**nawr**-suhn) **Expanse**-A field of stellar debris suspended in a gravity depression; this field of intense gravity was created by the competing pull of dual bodies: a white dwarf named Augustine on one end, and the Blanner Black Hole on the other end; the gravity depression trapped matter inside it, suspending it there, creating a natural barrier between the Old Territories (the region if space on Old Earth's side of the Expanse) and the New Territories (the region of space on Sharanda's side of the Expanse).

Old Territories-Settled region of space on Earth's side of the Norson Expanse

Oliver Towne-Team lead of the Horizon's crew; married; father of two young sons

Operations Center-A room deep within the bowels of Mount Efil where the highest level directors of the Trade Empire run their divisions and departments of the business; also called the Ops Center or the Command Center

Opus Star-The first star discovered by humans with satellite worlds capable of supporting human life; after settlement this system contained thirty-two colonized planets; neighbor to the Haron System

Opus System-See Opus Star

Oralti (awr-**al**-tee) **Crime Syndicate**-A mob-run criminal organization with main operations in the Sigma System; Gabriel Williams parents were born into this organization before fleeing it; run by Kasis Williams

Orff Stanlin-Masse's favorite senior chief petty officer; reminded Masse of himself when he was young; Masse grooming him for succession

Osis Oni (oh-**sis** oh-**nahy**)-The a massive battle during the Expansion Wars and the site of Georges Zorantham's last Stand

Petty Officer- The second highest rank achievable to enlisted personnel in the Republic's Navy; most naval men fall into this category in the Republic

Plumar (**ploo**-mahr) **Tree**-A tree only found on Sigma Eleven which has a special kind of pulp that prevents all translucency

Port-The left-hand side of a ship when facing forward

Project Manager-An expert in the planning, organizing and managing resources successfully and efficiently bring about specific goals; this person in the Trade Empire not specialize an in the discipline of any of the Empire's departments but instead specialized in work flow and business analysis, enabling the project manager to step into a project, analyze the project and then determine which resources should be pulled from various departments in order to complete said project

Ranis (**reyn**-is)- Planet located in the Ranis System; at war with neighboring planet Embuieck

Ranis (rey-nis) **System**-A star system which contained two inhabited planets, Ranis and Embuieck, which were at war with each other

Ronald Tse-The ATS Liahona's Courier

Rydell (rahy-**del**)-James Masse's personal pilot; captain of the Soulseeker

Schuelli (skoo-**wel**-lee) **Family**-The largest organized crime organization in the Sigma System; Zahn's employer

Scott Kilton-The Flagship's director of communications

SEAL-An acronym for an elite group soldiers in the navy who are highly trained in combat ad well as being specially trained to work under water and in space; this group of warriors is both highly respected and feared

Security Officer-Any one of a group of employees within the Argalian Trade Empire who worked within the security department of the business

Sharanda (shu-**ron**-duh)-Planet Located in the Galafon System; home to Mount Efil and the Argalian Trade Empire; this planet generated radiation field which was harmless to humans but disruptive anti-gravity technology

Sidearm-A one-handed gun which was holstered on the hip to one side

Sigma Commerce Bureau-The sole regulatory arm of the Galactic Democratic Republic in the New Territories; far too small to enforce regulations in a region this large

Sigma One-The epicenter of trade in the New Territories; Zahn's favored meeting place

Sigma System-A system of twenty four planets which all revolved around the Sigma Sun in an identical orbit resulting in all twenty four planets being almost identical; Sigma's planets were designated Sigma One through Sigma Twenty Four

Sigma Twelve-Home to Kasis Williams; the Oralti Crime Syndicate's base of operations

Soulseeker-Admiral James Masse's personal shuttle

Split Jackson-Manager of the Argalian Hover Skiff Horizon; Wife Tina; father of one grown daughter

Starboard-The right-hand side of a ship when facing forward

Steve Johnson-ATS Focus's project manager

Steven Parsons-Donahue's executive officer

The Blanner Black Hole-See Blanner Black Hole

The Republic-See Galactic Democratic Republic

Tina Jackson-Wife of Split Jackson; mother of one grown daughter

Trent Seigers-The Cryptography and Intelligence Center's managing Director

Viewer-A monitor on a bulkhead of a ship, usually very large

Zahn (**zahn**)-A top lieutenant of the Schuelli Crime Family organization who supplied many prominent Galactic figures including James Masse

Zorantham Box-A miniature, portable facsimile of a Zorantham compartment

Zorantham Compartment-A room built into ships to house the anti-gravity pulse generator for the soul purpose of dumping the generator, should it become damaged

Appendix B
Stellar Map

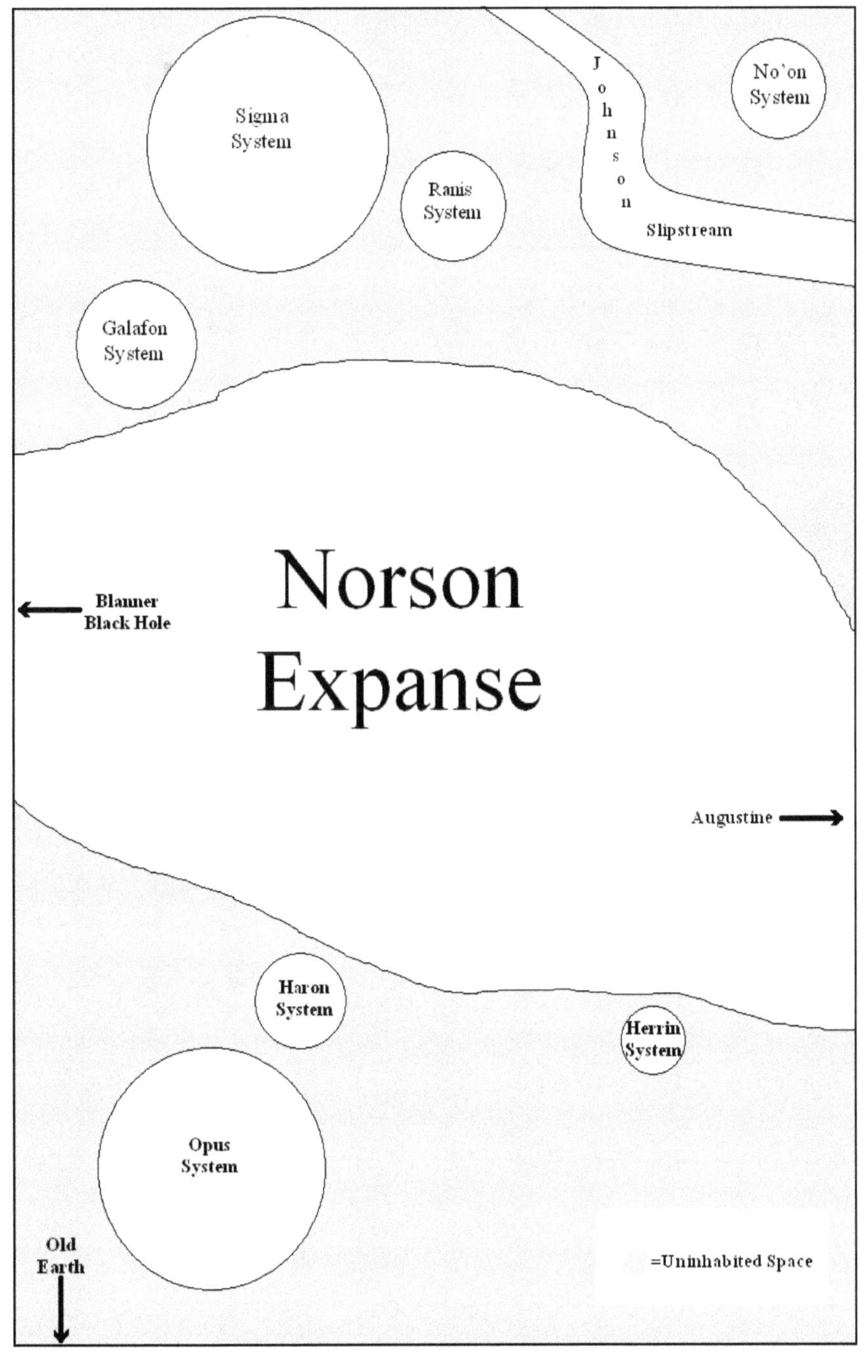

Appendix C
Timeline

T-200 yrs

T-200	Man begins colonization of space
t-39	Argolan Starts salvage business
T-36	Argolan and Masse split/Argolan and Angel marry
T-35	Faith born
T-33	Julian born
T-28	Man's first encounter with aliens/Julian orphaned
T-27	Julian and Gabriel Williams meet
T-26	Angel dies
T-25	Masse joins navy
T-15	Derelict stranded
T-6m	Focus left Sharanda
T-4m	Liahona left Sharanda
Today	Date of the beginning of this volume

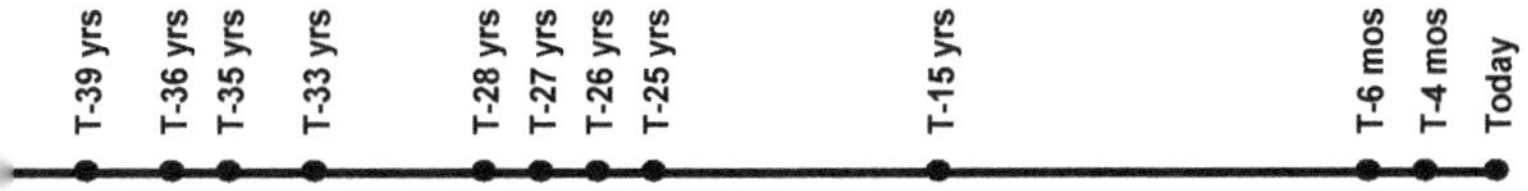

T-39 yrs
T-36 yrs
T-35 yrs
T-33 yrs
T-28 yrs
T-27 yrs
T-26 yrs
T-25 yrs
T-15 yrs
T-6 mos
T-4 mos
Today

Appendix D
Trade Empire Structure

The Argalian Trade Empire was broken into two basic types of structural units: Divisions and Departments.

Divisions

The Trade Empire's overall structure was broken segments called divisions. While The number of divisions comprising the Trade Empire fluctuated over time as needs for specific departments arose and waned, at the time period this volume covers, there it was broken into four divisions (shown in bold-face in the chart below) called: Imperial Legal Alliance, Cryptography and Intelligence Center, Fleet and Linguistics Foundation.

Departments

The divisions of the Empire were then broken into smaller units called department. Each department specialized in a specific skill set needed for the Efficient and effective operation of the Trade Empire. At the head of each department was a leader called director or manager. Each division differed in departmental structure from the overall Empire. However, the Fleet's departmental structure is very similar to the Empire's structure. Some, but not all, of the departments of the Empire were (shown in italics in the chart below): operations, science and engineering (includes machinists), security, dock engineering (fleet only), computers, communications, medical and project management. Role titles may vary from ship to ship. See Appendix E.

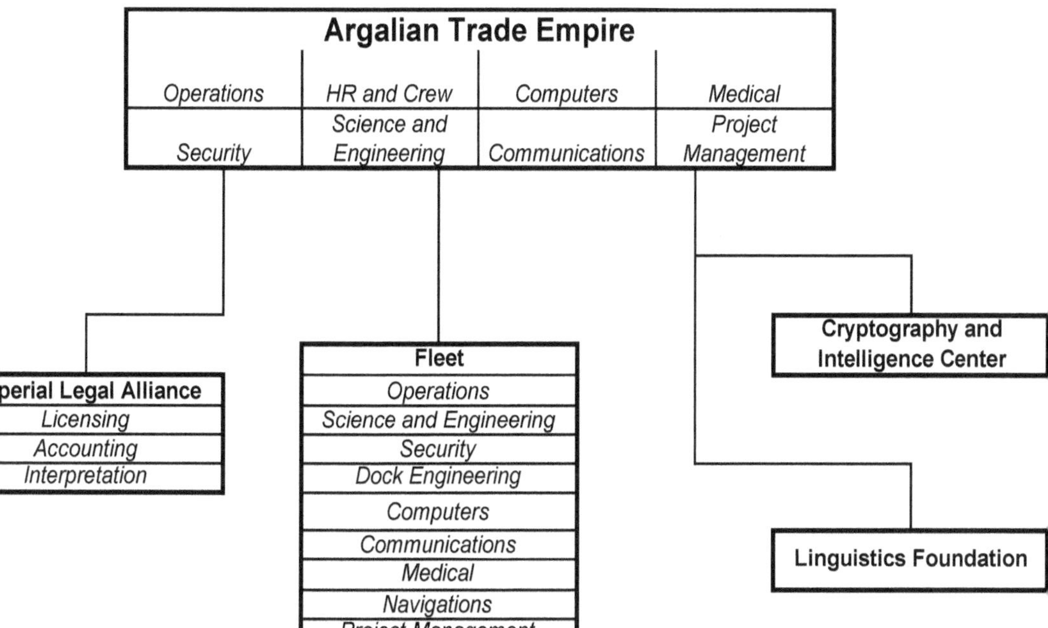

**For further information on the roles of departments and division please see the glossary as all of the divisions and many of the departments are explained there in greater depth

Appendix E
Crew and Organization Charts and Family Trees

Trade Empire Organization Charts

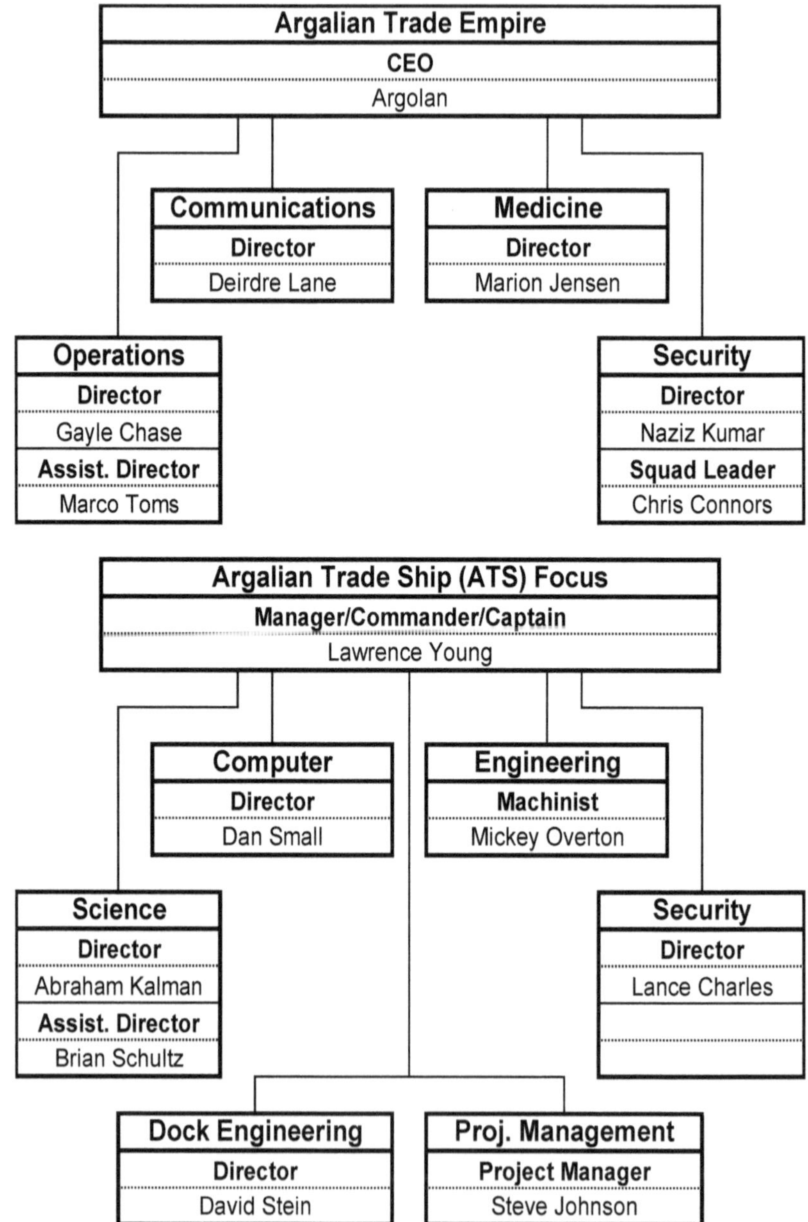

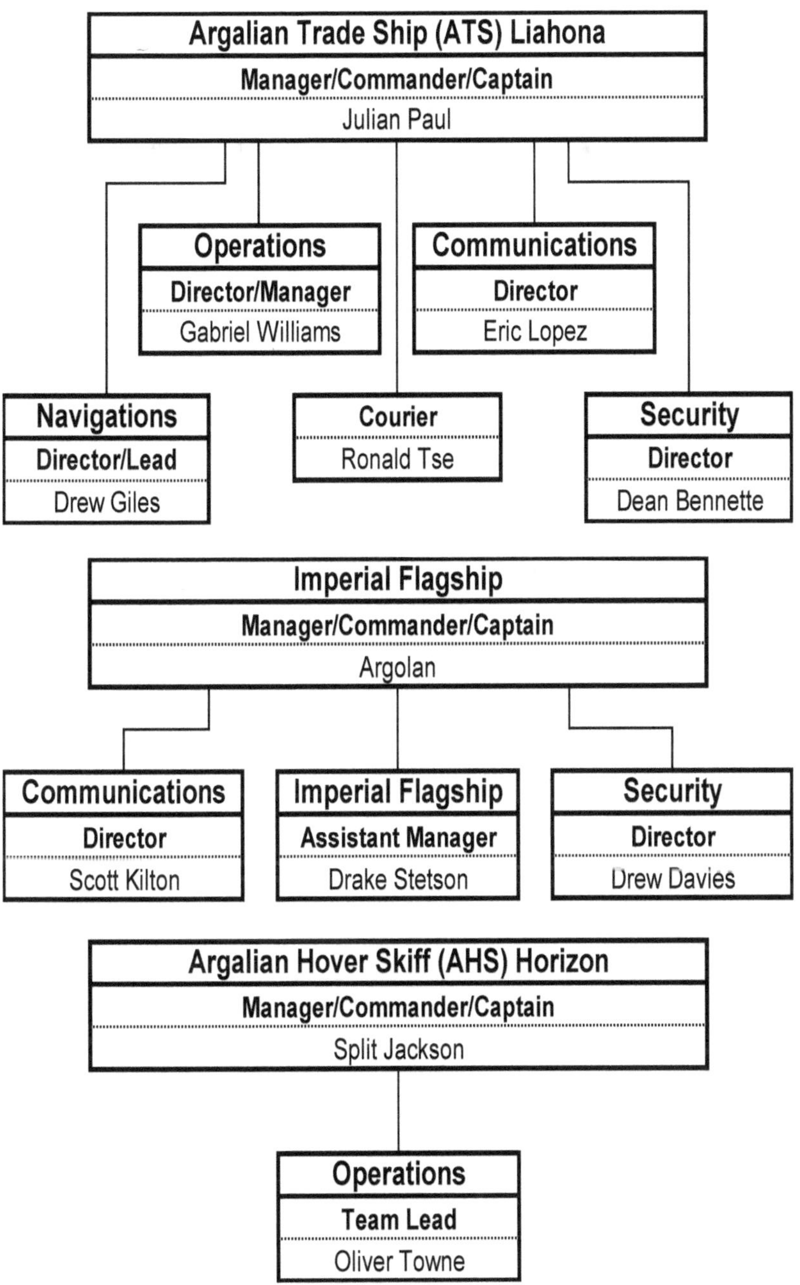

Argalian Trade Ship (ATS) Liahona
Manager/Commander/Captain
Julian Paul
Operations
Director/Manager
Gabriel Williams
Communications
Director
Eric Lopez
Navigations
Director/Lead
Drew Giles
Courier
Ronald Tse
Security
Director
Dean Bennette
Imperial Flagship
Manager/Commander/Captain
Argolan
Communications
Director
Scott Kilton
Imperial Flagship
Assistant Manager
Drake Stetson
Security
Director
Drew Davies
Argalian Hover Skiff (AHS) Horizon
Manager/Commander/Captain
Split Jackson
Operations
Team Lead
Oliver Towne

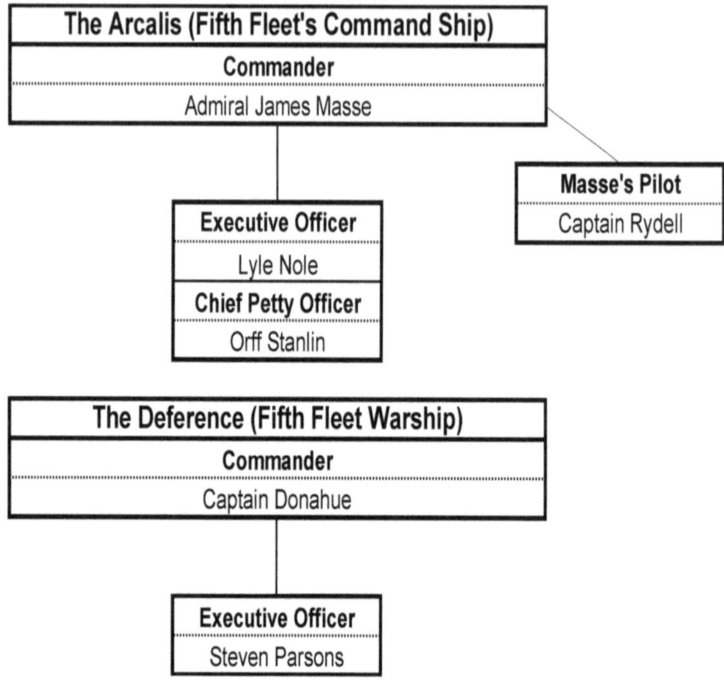

Argolan Family Tree

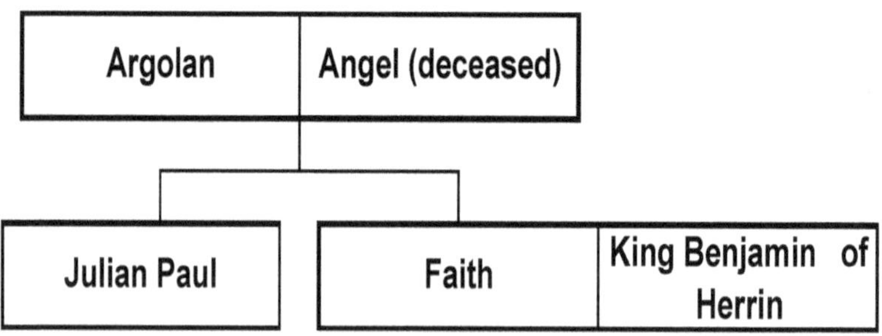